*The Twelfth
Pan Book
of Horror Stories*

Herbert van Thal has compiled a number of anthologies
which include some of the writings of James Agate, Ernest
Newman and Hilaire Belloc as well as a volume on Victorian
Travellers. He has also resuscitated the works of many
neglected Victorian writers. In 1971, his autobiography *The
Tops of the Mulberry Trees* will be published, as well as
The Music Lovers' Companion (with Gervase Hughes). He is
married to Phyllis Bayley, editor-in-chief of *Vanity Fair*,
and spends too much money on going to the Opera, collecting
French stamps and visiting his favourite countries, France
and Turkey.

D1437853

Also available in this series
The Pan Books of Horror Stories (Vols 1—11)

The Twelfth
Pan Book
Of Horror Stories

Edited by
Herbert van Thal

UNABRIDGED

PAN BOOKS LTD : LONDON

This collection first published 1971 by Pan Books Ltd,
33 Tothill Street, London S.W.1.

ISBN 0 330 02761 1

Printed and bound in England by
Hazell Watson & Viney Ltd,
Aylesbury, Bucks

CONTENTS

ACKNOWLEDGEMENTS

The Editor wishes to acknowledge the following permissions to quote from copyright material:

David Cass and his publishers, Macdonald & Company Limited of St Giles House, 49/50 Poland Street, London, W1A 2LG, for THE HUNTER from *The Cell (and other stories)*.

David Learmont c/o Pan Books Limited of 33 Tothill Street, London, SW1, for THE INSTANT DIVORCE.

Barry Martin and his agent, London Management Limited of 235/241 Regent Street, London, W1A 2JT, for IN MOTHER'S LOVING MEMORY.

Alan Hillery c/o Pan Books Limited for ASHES TO ASHES.

Patricia Highsmith and her publishers, William Heinemann Limited of 15 Queen Street, London, W1X 8BE, for THE TERRAPIN from *Eleven*.

Norman Kaufman and his agent, London Management Limited, for SERGEANT LACEY DEMONSTRATES.

James Jauncey c/o Pan Books Limited for BORDERLINE.

Robert Ashley c/o Pan Books Limited for PIECES OF MARY.

Frank Neate c/o Pan Books Limited for MISS FLETCHER'S PLUM TREE.

Martin Ricketts c/o Pan Books Limited for THE NURSERY CLUB.

Barry Martin and his agent, London Management Limited, for LAURA.

Rachel Kemper and her agent, London Management Limited, for THE DANCING SHOES.

Rosemary Timperley and her agent, Harvey Unna Limited of 14 Beaumont Mews, London, W1N 4HE, for THE PEG-DOLL.

T. H. McCormick c/o Pan Books Limited for MAN WITH A KNIFE.

The Hunter

David Case

It was a fine bright morning.

Ralph Conrad came out of the Bridge Hotel and shrugged his knapsack into a more comfortable position across his shoulders; smiled at the low sun and mopped his florid brow with a red polka-dot handkerchief. There were several motor-cars in the parking lot, but no traffic on the road at this early hour, and Ralph was very much at peace with himself. He felt especially peaceful because the hotel clerk, befuddled and sleepy, had made a ten-shilling error in Ralph's favour, and Ralph was of a thrifty nature. That was why he was on a walking tour of Dartmoor. When he had first retired several years before, he had contemplated taking up golf for exercise, but the expense of that game had troubled him more than his inability to predict the direction the ball would travel, and since the exercise gained by walking through open country was certainly equal to that gained by pursuing an elusive little white ball through various frustrating hazards and roughs, Ralph had forsaken golf in favour of leisurely walking tours. He had walked through the Lake District and Northern Wales and this was the third day of his tour of Dartmoor. He planned, vaguely, to walk on the Continent some day, but that wasn't definite or immediate; it was a thing to think about rather than do, because Ralph liked the English life he was accustomed to, liked to have a destination where he would find a hot meal and a comfortable bed, familiar food and conversation in a familiar language beside an open fire when he relaxed after a long day's tramp. He had also heard that the Continent was frightfully expensive.

Ralph walked up to the highway and along the shoulder for

several hundred yards, anxious to progress some distance before the clerk discovered his error. He wore stout shoes and carried a walking stick with an electric torch built into the handle; he had an Ordnance survey map and knew how to cross rough country without getting lost, impressing the landscape upon his mind and using his wristwatch and the sun to estimate the points of the compass. This ability pleased him, since it had saved him the expense of purchasing a compass. He carried a light lunch and a Thermos of coffee and had planned to arrive comfortably at his next stop around dinnertime. His route had been meticulously laid out on the map, and presently he turned from the road and set out across the moors.

The sun was hot. Ralph thought that perhaps it would be unpleasantly warm later in the day, and he walked rather more quickly than usual so that he could slow down later, if the heat made it necessary. His route took him along the crest of a hill. A narrow stream wound through the marshy land below on the left, and a higher ridge of land studded with rocky tors bordered his path on the right. The tors were individually marked on his excellent map and he judged his progress by them, admiring the formations as he studied the terrain. This was some of the loveliest and most desolate country in England, and Ralph appreciated it greatly. He was all alone. There was no noise of motor-car or factory to disturb his tranquillity, no scent of petrol or fumes of industry to overwhelm the dry perfume of the heather, no black smoke twisted against the fluffy white clouds. The stream twinkled through the mossy ground and his heavy shoes crunched on the coarse tufts of grass, squelching occasionally when he moved too low on the slope. Ralph drew deep breaths of clean air into his lungs. He had stopped smoking years before, when the rising tax on tobacco had made the expense greater than the satisfaction, but this pure air was even better than nicotine, and he complimented himself on the will-power it had taken to forsake cigarettes, not even considering the economies of the sacrifice.

When he had been walking for nearly an hour, Ralph came to a low, flat rock and sat down to rest. He scraped some mud from his shoes with the tip of his stick and unscrewed the cap

from his Thermos jug, poured some coffee into the cap and
was about to drink when he noticed something in the reeds
near the stream. He lowered the cup and looked harder. He
couldn't quite make out what it was. The sun was bright and
he had to squint and shield his eyes. He wished that he had
sunglasses, but didn't think the frequency of sunlight justified
buying them; he thought that he really should have a pair of
field-glasses and wondered what they might cost in a pawn
shop.

Ralph didn't want to move down the hill because the land was
damp and marshy there and he hated to get his feet wet, but he
was basically a curious man, and who knew but what the object
might be something valuable? He knew he would never forgive
himself if he walked on without investigating.

He climbed up on the rock to get a higher angle, but still
couldn't make out what it was. It looked almost like a man, he
thought, but that could hardly be possible. A man wouldn't be
lying in that swampy ground, surely. Not with the exorbitant
prices that dry cleaners charged these days.

He climbed down again and finished his coffee, still undecided
whether he should risk the dampness, replaced the Thermos
jug in his pack, looked ahead, then shrugged and started
cautiously down the incline.

The lower he went, the softer the ground became. His feet
squished as the mud sucked at them, his stick sank deeply and
gave little support. Reeds replaced the coarse grass, and he
found it more difficult to keep the object in sight since, although
he was closer to it, he no longer had the advantage of elevation.
He was just about to deny his curiosity and return to the high
ground when he came upon a shoe.

His eyes narrowed as he looked at it. It was quite definitely
a shoe, sunk well down in the muck. He crouched and pried
it up with his stick; lifted it between thumb and forefinger. It
had apparently been sucked off as its owner walked or ran
through the mud and abandoned there. Ralph turned it about
and saw that it was in fairly good condition, a bit run down at
the heel but with a great deal of wear left in it; measured it
beside his own shoe and decided it would be too small for him.

He couldn't understand this. Someone had recently passed this way in a hurry – such a great hurry that he had not paused to retrieve his shoe. Such reckless abandoning of a useful article was beyond Ralph's comprehension. He looked around, hoping perhaps to find the other shoe. They might fit him, after all. There was no other shoe, but he noticed an indentation in the ground and moved to it. It looked like a footprint. Water had seeped into it and the edge had crumbled. There was another similar indentation beyond, and Ralph moved in that direction, the shoe still gripped gingerly in his fingers. He was very curious indeed now. After all, one shoe was useless to its owner, and there seemed a reasonably good chance that the mate had also been abandoned.

Then he saw the object that had first caught his attention. The footprints led in that direction, and it looked like a bundle of rags glimpsed through the reeds. Perhaps, he thought, a complete outfit of clothing cast off in some moment of insanity.

Ralph approached warily; halted abruptly.

It was certainly a pile of clothing, and from one end protruded a human foot. Ralph stared at the foot. It wore a sock but no shoe. Ralph looked at the shoe he held and then back at the foot. He felt confused and dazed. He had never come upon a situation like this before in all his rambles; he felt that he should do something but had no precedent to help him decide what steps were called for. After a few moments he took a firmer grip on his stick and advanced with resolution and determination, until he was standing beside the body. One arm was outflung, the other hidden in the shredded rags. The rags were darkly stained with blood and the coat had been pulled above the shoulders so that it covered the man's head.

'I say there,' Ralph said.

There was no reply.

'I say, my man. Are you all right?'

The rags were silent.

Ralph took a deep breath. He hated to get involved in difficulties that didn't concern him, but saw that he had no choice. He crouched and drew the coat down so he could see the man's face.

And then the peaceful countryside was shattered by his scream.

The man had no head.

And Ralph had never encountered such a thing before . . .

2

John Wetherby was in the habit of dining several times a week at his club in St James's. He invariably ate the same well-balanced meal, drank the same full-bodied burgundy, and then went into the bar for the same excellent brandy and Havana cigar. But Wetherby was not a creature of thoughtless habit. He simply found this a comfortable and satisfying routine, and saw no reason to alter it, any more than he would have changed his tailor or the rather outdated cut of his suits.

Wetherby's club was The Venturers. He had been a member for many years, and, not being plagued by a compulsion to join and belong, he subscribed to no other club. The Venturers had, however, changed considerably over the years. It had become fashionable rather than purposeful and the requirements for membership were based more on social standing than accomplishment. It was no longer the sort of club that Wetherby would have selected for himself, but he didn't contemplate a change; he doubted if any new club would prove more suitable and thought, if he thought of it at all, that it was more likely the tempo of the world rather than the tone of his club which had changed. Or perhaps, he sighed at the idea that he himself had changed with age, and failed to keep up with life.

There were times when he regretted this, such as when he walked into the bar and saw the younger members lounging about in well-cut suits and seldom-cut hair, with pretence and affectation. Wetherby was a tolerant man. He could regret without resenting. But he felt a definite longing for former days, when there had been mutual interest among the members – adventures to be recalled over the brandy or, better still, further adventures to be planned and anticipated. But this was in the past. It had been a long time since Wetherby had had an adventure, and even if some of the old members had been present, the conversation would of necessity have dwelt on the past; it would have been a sad pleasure, recalling things that could no longer be.

Wetherby glanced around the dining-room. There was no one there he knew. There seldom was now. Of all the friends and companions he could recall from better days, only Byron had not succumbed to the advance of age; only Byron, timelessly pursuing his curious theories of life and death, might have had some new tale to tell. But Byron never came to London now. He still lived a life of adventure, and had no need to reminisce about the past. Wetherby admired Byron without envying him, approved of the man without approving of his methods. It had been nearly ten years since he had last seen Byron and Wetherby vividly recalled that evening.

They had been drinking brandy at the bar. Byron had just returned from Africa and Wetherby had just decided it was time for him to give up big-game hunting. They had talked for a while about the last expedition they'd been on together, in north-west Canada, and then Wetherby had mentioned his decision to retire. Byron had been annoyed, almost angry, about it. Wetherby himself was rather sad, but the decision was unalterable. He was no longer young, his eyes and his reflexes had lost the sharpness required. He had spent his youth practising a passion for hunting; but now his youth was over, and Wetherby did not care to pursue danger when he might not enjoy it, might prove a liability rather than an asset to his companions.

But hunting, to Byron, was far more than a pleasure or a pastime; it was more than a passion, it was a philosophy of life. Byron had become excited, trying to convince Wetherby he was making a grave mistake in deciding to live a life of comfort in London. Byron's voice was resonant and deep, and with the fervour of his words, he began speaking loudly, gesturing widely.

Several of the younger members had been standing beside them at the bar, and they looked on with interest, obviously amused by the intensity of Byron's speech, undoubtedly considering him an anachronism in their modern world. One of them, a large young man with an insolent face, drew closer. A leader of the liberal new aristocracy. He winked at his companions and hovered beside Byron. He was so close that Byron, despite his impassioned monologue, could not fail to notice him.

Byron paused in the middle of a sentence and turned towards the young man; stared at him. Byron's eyes were piercing, he did not stare the way a man stares in a city, he stared as one does, with full concentration and awareness, in the jungle. He said nothing. The young man tried to return the gaze but his civilized eyes faltered, and he sought refuge in words.

'I couldn't help but overhear you, sir,' he said. He had a cultured voice and emphasized the 'sir'.

Byron didn't seem to hear.

'You are, I understand, a big-game hunter?'

Byron said nothing. Wetherby said, 'That is correct, young man. We both are.'

But the man wasn't interested in Wetherby. His face had become flushed under Byron's eyes.

'Perhaps you can tell me – something I've always wondered – what on earth is the pleasure that full-grown and presumably intelligent men get out of murdering defenceless animals?'

It was not the thing to say to Byron.

Wetherby was angry himself. Tolerance has limits. The young man's cohorts moved closer, grinning behind their champion. But Byron still said nothing. He continued to stare but, slowly, his expression shifted until he was regarding the man in precisely the same manner as one might some foul object upon which one has inadvertently trod.

The young man became intensely uncomfortable. His friends were expecting him to make some brilliant comment which would terminate the encounter, and yet he could not force himself to look at Byron's eyes.

'I don't mean to intrude, of course,' he said. 'But tell me —' Encouraged by the sound of his own educated voice, he smiled again. 'Tell me, is it a sense of power? Of accomplishment? Some regression to the past, when killing was an honourable and necessary thing?'

'I cannot tell you,' Byron said.

'I thought not,' the man said. He started to turn away, his lips smirking. His friends grinned at their clever comrade.

'However, I could show you,' Byron said.

The young man turned back, surprised. Byron had moved out from the bar. He was smiling, too. They say a tiger smiles and a hyena laughs, but perhaps they are mistaken.

'I beg your pardon?' the young man said.

'The pleasure I get from killing,' Byron said. 'I could show you just what it is. I think it would be a very great pleasure, showing you, although I doubt you would die with the nobility of an animal.'

Everyone was very quiet. The young man's lips parted, but he said nothing. His friends no longer smiled. They had seen something very dark in Byron's eyes, something they would never comprehend. After a moment the young man turned away; Byron shrugged and leaned on the bar again. Wetherby let his breath out slowly. He had seen Byron kill, and he knew that face very well. It was not a face one could forget. The young men left very soon.

'I thought, for a moment —' Wetherby said.

Byron nodded.

'It would have been so easy,' he said.

Wetherby didn't doubt it.

That was Byron . . .

The waiter brought the bill, knowing from long experience that Wetherby would not take brandy at the table. Wetherby signed it and stood up; headed for the bar, through the solid, oak-panelled rooms. He was a tall man with steel-grey hair and angular features, wearing a new suit which was tailored so well that it looked old. Middle age may have dulled his vision and blunted his reflexes, but a life of civilized comfort had not harmed him noticeably. He was lean and hard and straight, and weighed exactly the same as he had on his last hunting trip, with Byron in Canada. Wetherby was thinking about Byron as he entered the bar.

It was a strange coincidence.

Detective Superintendent Justin Bell was drinking a pint of beer at the bar. He had a brick-red face and a nondescript grey suit and looked very much like a policeman. He raised his glass and Wetherby joined him. He was pleased to see him; Bell was one of the older members, and Wetherby had seconded his application, following a tongue-in-cheek discussion over whether police work qualified as adventurous endeavour and, therefore, met the requirements of membership. That was before the rules had been changed, when The Venturers had a purpose. Bell was well liked and had the proper outlook and temperament for the club, and so he had been admitted to the rolls, even though his occupation was suspect.

'Hello, John,' Bell said.

'How are you, Justin?'

'Tired.'

'You haven't been here for quite a while.'

'No time. I envy your life of ease. Always have. It's a fortunate man who can retire from a life of pleasure to a life of relaxation without a period of work in between.'

Wetherby laughed. He had always felt the same way; had, without the slightest taint of snobbery, considered himself very lucky to have been born wealthy.

'Drink?' he asked.

Bell finished his beer and slid the glass across the bar. The barman wore a wine-coloured jacket and was very efficient and polite; although young, he was able to distinguish between the old-established Venturers and the fashionable new members; knew the difference between dignity and familiarity. Wetherby had a brandy and Bell had another pint of beer. His preference for beer had begun to extend his waistline slightly, but that merely made him look more like an efficient lawman.

'It's good to see you,' Wetherby said.

'As a matter of fact, I came here to see you. Thought you'd be here.'

'Good Lord. Not about that parking ticket?'

They laughed at the private reference to a slight bending of a minor law.

After a moment, Bell said, 'I need your advice, John.'

'Whatever for?'

'Possibly a murder.'

Wetherby blinked. Bell drank.

'At least, we're treating it as murder. I don't really know that it is.'

'Surely there's no advice I can give you on that?'

'Perhaps not. Not if it actually is murder.'

'This sounds very mysterious,' Wetherby said. He began to fill his pipe very carefully. He hadn't tasted the brandy yet.

'Well, it is, in a way. I expect you've read something about it. The headless body on Dartmoor. I believe that was how the newspapers billed it.'

'Oh yes. Yes, I did see something about that. A bit out of your territory, isn't it?'

'Well, there are curious aspects. It baffled the chief constable down there and he asked for assistance. Good judge, I'd say. It baffles me, too. Anyway, the commissioner assigned Thurlow and me to the case. I've just come back from there. Came back to see you specifically.'

Wetherby had the briar filled; he lighted it, tamped it down and touched the flame again. He smoked Afrikander and, like most good tobaccos, it didn't smell as good as it tasted. Bell lit a cigarette.

'Well?' Wetherby asked.

'There's a very distinct possibility that this killing was the work of some animal. Everything, bar one curious fact, points to that. And I can't think of anyone who would be more qualified to advise me on that. One way or the other.'

'I see,' Wetherby said. He tasted the brandy. 'What sort of animal did you have in mind?'

'None. I don't know a damn thing about animals and Thurlow knows less. My wife had a cat once, but it ran away. And I think there's a mole in my garden. That's the lot.'

Wetherby smiled.

'I thought maybe you could tell me by examining the marks on the body and the plaster casts of the tracks.'

Wetherby nodded. 'Yes, I should think I could,' he said. 'Were the tracks plain?'

'Not very.'

'Well, I can certainly get an idea what sort of animal it was, if nothing else. A carnivore, I assume?'

'I don't know. The body wasn't devoured, if that's anything to go on. But it was savaged. Mangled. The police doctor swears that only a wild and savage animal could have done it. In fact, we would have been definite on that, except for the one curious fact – the one the papers all stressed, of course – the remarkable incident of the decapitation, as Doyle might have said. That was what confused the local police. The chief is a doddery old sort anyhow, all vintage port and confusion.' Bell gestured with his pint.

'We never did find the head,' he added.

Wetherby thought for a few moments, drawing on his pipe. It was rather like old times, pondering a problem at this bar, although the conversation on all sides dealt more with fashion and art than life and death.

'So this animal – if it was an animal – was something powerful enough to tear a man's head off, eh?'

Bell shrugged.

'In England? It seems doubtful. Possibly a pack of wild dogs, but I shouldn't think so. You've checked with all the zoos and circuses about an escaped carnivore, of course?'

Bell looked pained.

Wetherby said, 'Of course. Sorry, Justin.'

'It's a bit more confusing than that, actually,' Bell said. 'The head wasn't torn off. Not the way an animal would tear a body. The body was ripped and clawed, almost shredded, but the head was severed quite neatly.'

Wetherby frowned through the tobacco haze.

'That would mean enormous strength. Some animal powerful enough to take the skull in its jaws and yank it off with one explosive jerk. And hold the body down at the same time.'

'As clean as a knife or a guillotine,' Bell said. His face was clouded as he recalled the corpse. 'What animal could have done that?'

'I don't know. Perhaps if I saw the tracks. A buffalo, for instance, might be able to hook a man's head off with one stroke of its horns. But if the body was clawed – I don't know, Justin. Perhaps some madman with a weapon that inflicted wounds like talons?'

'No. They were claw marks, all right. Fangs, too. No man could have done that.'

'Well, I'll be glad to help you in any way I can.'

'Could you come down to Dartmoor with me. On expenses, of course. The ground was soft and we've got some fair casts of the prints. You might recognize them.'

Bell remembered that he, too, was on expenses. He signalled for another round.

'It's been a long time since I've done any tracking. Still, I suppose that knowledge doesn't leave entirely. I could give it a try.'

Bell was unfolding a map. He spread it out on the bar, holding one corner down with his beer glass. Several of the young members looked over in interest. It had been a long time since a map had been studied at that bar. Wetherby leaned over and Bell pointed with a thick finger.

'The body was found —' The finger described a circle, then jabbed on to the map. 'Here. Beside this stream.'

Wetherby nodded, automatically forming an image of the terrain as he studied the contour map. Then, as his area of interest widened, he looked surprised; he took the pipe from his mouth, frowning.

'You knew Byron, didn't you?'

'Oh yes.'

'Why, he lives there.' Wetherby looked at the map again. It was remarkably detailed. 'His house can't be more than a mile from where the body was discovered.'

'Yes, I know.'

'You could have saved yourself a trip by asking his advice. Or isn't he in the country?'

Bell looked uncomfortable.

'Actually, I did go to Byron,' he said. 'He wasn't interested in helping me. Always was a strange sort. The whole damn thing seemed to amuse him and he said something about it being just as well to kill people off, to counterbalance the popu-

lation explosion. Said there were too damn many people in the
world as it was.'

'Yes, that's Byron. But surely he would have been interested
in a challenge of this nature?'

'He was interested in the plaster casts, all right. Looked at
them for quite a while, and I thought he had an idea what
might have made them. But then he just shrugged and wouldn't
venture an opinion. In fact, he suggested that I see you. Said
you'd be more interested and concerned about what happened
to humanity.' Bell paused. 'Of course, I intended to see
you anyway. I only went to Byron's first because it was
closer.'

Wetherby grinned.

'Rather like hunting tigers in Africa,' he said. 'Are you sure
you checked the zoo?'

They laughed and Wetherby bought a round of drinks.

'It certainly isn't like Byron to pass up an opportunity like
this,' Wetherby said. 'Not that he ever had much regard for
life, human or otherwise – he was more concerned with death
– but if he thought this was a dangerous animal he'd be out
with his gun. The more dangerous, the faster he'd be out. Last
time I saw him he cursed me for giving up danger and living
in town. Either he doesn't think it's an animal or, perhaps, he
didn't want to help the authorities. That seems more likely.
He might be out looking for the killer on his own. And, knowing Byron, he'll find it. Still, as you say, he's a strange fellow
and I don't pretend to understand him.'

'Will you come down with me, John?'

'You could have brought the casts with you.'

'Yes, I considered it. But I'd like you down there. This is
one of those killings without apparent motive which may never
be solved. And the worst thing about them is they are so often
repeated. Whether it was a man or a beast, there seems a good
chance it will kill again.'

'And you'd like me there if it does.'

'Exactly. If anyone could track the killer, it would be you.
And if, God forbid, it kills again, it would be better if you had a
fresh trail. If we ever solve this, I think it more likely to be by

physical means, rather than deduction. As Doyle surely never said.'

Wetherby nodded. There was nothing to keep him in London, and the thought of getting into the open again was pleasant. He thought it might be nice to see Byron again, too. Byron and he had shared danger many times, and if that was the sole bond between them, it was a strong bond.

'All right, Justin. I'll come.'

Bell folded the map and stuffed it in his pocket. His suit bulged with the encumbrance of such stuffings, and Wetherby wondered, smiling, if there was a magnifying glass somewhere in those drooping pockets. They sat at a table in the corner and had a last drink, making their plans to go down to Dartmoor in the morning. More through habits of conversation, than because Wetherby needed the information, Bell filled in the details of the killing. There was a great deal and yet there wasn't enough. The man who discovered the body was certainly not connected in any way other than circumstance. The body, with some difficulty, had been identified. It was an old fellow named Randal who had lived a hermitic life in the area, and who had been arrested for poaching several times. It seemed likely that he'd been doing just that when his death found him. The tracks made it obvious that Randal had been walking along the firm ground higher up the hill, and had fled towards the stream when he had seen his killer. He had almost reached the water when it overtook him, and he had died at the same spot where his body had been found. There was no sign that he had been injured as he ran, as might have been the case had an animal worried him, snapping at his heels until he was brought down. As soon as his killer caught him, it killed him. There were some signs of short but violent struggle, Randal had rolled over several times and his fingernails were splintered. His clothing had been torn to shreds, but his pockets hadn't been emptied, and contained four shillings and half an ounce of rolling tobacco. Randal had been an amusing local character, an eccentric with no known enemies, and the killing seemed entirely pointless.

Bell stopped talking; shook his head.

'It was a particularly ugly death,' he said. 'I don't suppose it was any worse for poor old Randal than any number of deaths might have been, but I'll tell you, John – I don't relish the thought of seeing another corpse like this.'

Bell shook his head again.

He was going to.

3

Damn me, thought Brian Hammond. Damn me for a fool.

He leaned forward, both hands clamped on the steering wheel, and peered out through the rain-washed windscreen. It was hard to see the road. The wipers left curved blurs across the glass and the headlights shot pale beams futilely against the trees. Hammond's dark-jowled face, illuminated in the green glow of the dashlights, was angry and worried. He was a salesman but he looked like a merchant seaman. He had, in fact, been a merchant seaman when he was younger, but then he had looked more like a salesman. It was the type of face destined to foil enterprise. Brian sat rigidly in the seat, a cigar clamped in his teeth, as he steered along the dark and winding country lane.

How did I manage to miss that turning? he wondered. And why don't they put signposts on these blasted roads. How do they expect a man to find his way without any signs? All the taxes I pay, and I can't even find a road sign. Not to mention a petrol station.

His eyes turned down to the fuel gauge. The needle was hovering on the empty mark.

Damn this God-forsaken area, he thought. All the local country bumpkins are asleep, no one to ask directions, haven't even seen a house. Can't see anything anyway in this damn rain. Don't think I've got petrol for more than another mile or so. Damn car drinks petrol. Ought to get a smaller car, except then I wouldn't have any room for all these damn samples. Not that it would matter much. Haven't sold a damn thing all day. The boss will squawk like a stuck pig, too, damn him. How does he expect me to sell electronic equipment in this bloody area? Nothing here but sheep. These yokels probably never even heard of electricity and I'm supposed to sell them equipment. Ought to give Cornwall independence, and then give them Dartmoor. Get rid of the damn place.

He turned a sharp corner and the lane rose ahead, dark and deserted.

That damn Ed Davis is working in London, too, he thought. Probably made plenty of sales today and now he's celebrating in the West End. Lucky bastard. Probably drinking champagne. Damn him, anyway. Why should he get all the choice territory just because he's been with the company longer? It isn't fair.

The car banged against the high shoulder of the road and Hammond snarled as he turned the wheel. He felt very sorry for himself. If there was any justice in the world he would be home by his fireside watching television while his wife made him a nice cup of tea. I wonder what my wife is doing now? he thought. She hates it when I have to travel. 'Course, she knows I can't get into any trouble down here. I guess she just hates to have me be away. Real passionate, that wife of mine. I wonder if she went up to the pub tonight? He bit hard on the cigar. Ah, she wouldn't go to the pub alone. She's not like that. Faithful, my wife. But that damn Humphries is always trying to flirt with her in the pub. Caught her smiling back at him once, too. I'll bet she's gone up to the pub to flirt with Humphries.

Hammond looked at his watch. It was past closing time.

No, she isn't in the pub, he thought. Must be home. I'd phone her if this damn place had any phone boxes. All the taxes I pay and I can't even find a phone box when I want one. But if I phoned and she wasn't home — Ah, she'd be home. I wonder if that damn Humphries is home with her? If I thought for one minute that she —

Hammond shook his head and squinted into the black night. The wipers skimmed ineffectively over a film of water and the car veered from side to side. The samples slid around on the back seat, the tyres hummed, the foul cigar smoke hung heavy in the air. He had to drive slowly and it seemed he'd been driving for a very long time. And then the motor coughed and sputtered.

Oh no, Hammond thought.

The motor gulped the last ounce of petrol and the car glided to a silent stop. Brian sat scowling behind the wheel, thinking of the futility of joining the AA when he couldn't phone for aid. His mood was black. He felt sure that his wife was with that rogue Humphries and that he was going to lose his job because he'd sold nothing. He relighted his cigar and puffed away, wondering what to do. He had no idea where he was, and saw little sense in trying to walk somewhere in the dark. The rain was falling heavily. Hammond sighed and resigned himself to a cramped night in the car. The battery wasn't new, and he turned the lights off. But the road was narrow and dark, and it was dangerous without lights in the remote possibility that another car might come along. He opened the glove box and took out the flasher, pulled his collar up and opened the door. The rain singled him out, finding chinks in the armour of his clothing, and he swore to himself as he walked back a few yards and placed the flasher on its tripod behind the car. He snapped it on and the red light began to blink. It lighted the trees with an eerie effect. It was very unreal. He stood there for a moment, watching the trees appear red and black, red and black. His cigar had gone out again and a loose leaf curled down. He was looking at the trees and then he was looking at something else that came out from the trees. For a moment he merely looked surprised, then his eyes widened and the cigar dropped as his mouth opened to scream. But only a whimper of fear came out.

Hammond turned and ran, without thinking where he was heading. He ran past his car, blind and dumb with terror. He ran for perhaps fifty yards before it caught him . . .

4

John Wetherby sat by the dying embers of his fire, drinking a last brandy and considering the things that Bell had told him. It was a comfortable room. The grandfather clock ticked with soothing regularity in the corner, the pendulum catching flashes of reflection through the arc. The walls were lined with beautifully bound books, the carpet was deep and soft, heavy tapestries were drawn across the wide windows. But, Wetherby, in his thoughts, was dissociated from this room; was back in a former way of life, with a different pattern of reason. He was trying to anticipate what he would learn in Dartmoor, to predict before seeing them what the tracks might be, what animal could be responsible for the unusual aspects of the case. And, not the least remarkable aspect, to one who knew Byron, was the man's failure to rise to a challenge of this nature, even for purely selfish reasons. That was a mystery in itself, quite apart from the killing. Byron was a man who had always gone out of his way to find a challenge; he invariably did things in the most risky and dangerous fashion simply to create a challenge against his life itself. And, the older he got, the greater this need became. As Wetherby began to feel himself slowing down and relied on his experience to do things the safest and easiest way, Byron had seemed compelled to increase the difficulties of the tasks he took in hand. Wetherby had hunted with Byron many times, in India and Africa and once, the last time, in the wilderness of northern Canada. He vividly recalled that Canada expedition. Never had Byron taken a risk that seemed more pointless – danger for the pure sake of danger. Byron wanted a Kodiak bear, and he wanted it alone, insisted that Wetherby wait at a distance too great to be of any possible aid. And, although he had splendid guns, he had borrowed a ·30–06 from their guide, a good gun but much too light for the job; a gun he had not even fired before. Wetherby had protested in vain. Byron was not a man to listen to reason, much less argument, and so Wetherby had waited. He could still recall the tenseness he had felt on that memorable day. He had been waiting on a hill, surrounded by evergreens. It was autumn. The forest was burning with colour, trees ablaze in reds and yellows. The ground was crisp with early frost and a chill wind stirred from the north. Wetherby had watched Byron's figure diminish as he strode away moving towards where they knew the bear was waiting. Byron looked very casual, but that was deceptive. His red and black plaid shooting coat blended against the background of leaves. He looked very small, drawing farther away, towards the dense thicket where his quarry waited. He was already out of effective range, Wetherby would be helpless from where he stood. He gripped his rifle, but knew it was useless. Byron was completely on his own.

Byron was almost at the thicket when the bear reared up. Even at that distance, Wetherby was astounded at the monster's size. He saw Byron raise the rifle, a tiny manikin only a few yards from those fourteen hundred pounds of power and fury. The bear's head seemed larger than Byron, towering three feet above him as the beast rose on its hind legs. And then the bear was off balance, twisting around and down, thrashing in death, and it seemed a long time later that the sharp crack of the rifle reached Wetherby's ears. Byron had turned and raised the gun, motioning for Wetherby to advance. Wetherby had advanced.

Byron was smiling, looking down at the bear. It was a smile of pure pleasure. He had fired once, as the bear roared in warning, and the slug had gone up through the roof of that terrible mouth and into the brain. It had not emerged. There was no mark on the trophy.

'A fine shot,' Wetherby said.

'I couldn't very well have missed at that range. Couldn't afford to, either.'

'Not with that,' Wetherby said, looking at the rifle.

'Oh, a ·30–06 will kill a bear if the shot is placed right.'

'Obviously.'

Byron was amused. 'Why should I use a heavier weapon than I need? That just makes a man sloppy. That ·402 you carry, for instance. You could have dropped it even with a bad shot, broken its shoulder or shattered its leg and then finished it at your leisure. That isn't hunting, John. That isn't living. That's not the way to keep life and give death. You're a fine hunter and a splendid shot, but your values are wrong.'

'Perhaps,' Wetherby said with a mixture of admiration and annoyance, half understanding what Byron meant, and resenting an understanding he did not follow.

'Not perhaps. A categorical fact. An objective truth.'

'But if you hadn't made a perfect shot – if something had happened, if the bear had shifted just a few inches as you fired – you couldn't have stopped a wounded charge with a rifle that light. Even if your second shot had been perfect, it would have killed you through sheer impetus and reflex.'

Byron smiled again. This was a different smile.

'No,' he said. 'But that's a moot point.'

Wetherby raised his eyebrows.

Byron tossed the rifle to him. Wetherby caught it. He knew, absolutely, what Byron meant then. He worked the lever. The empty shell ejected. There had been only one bullet in the rifle.

'You're mad,' Wetherby said.

And Byron laughed in mad delight . . .

Later, by the campfire, Byron had been in a thoughtful, philosophical mood. His immediate pleasure had faded, and he seemed possessed with a need to share his attitudes with Wetherby. They were alone. Their guide was skinning the bear where it had fallen; it was too huge to move. Wetherby was still greatly disturbed by the enormous risk Byron had taken; a risk that seemed to border on the unbalance of madness.

'Can't you understand, John?' Byron said. He was almost pleading for understanding.

'I don't know. I see the emotion of it – even the accomplishment. But it's suicidal, Byron. Some day —'

Byron silenced him with a gesture. His eyes were bright in the firelight.

'Danger, John. Only in danger are we alive. Only by risking our lives can we appreciate them. How much fuller our existence is than that of a city man, castrated by civilization, emasculated by society and safety. There is no life there, no danger and no joy, no risk and, therefore, nothing to risk. And we give life as we take it, John. That bear was never more alive than the instant before the bullet entered his brain. If we, the hunters, are more alive and aware, then it must work even more so for the hunted. I love the things I kill, John. The things that would kill me if I was too slow, if I failed to observe, if my shot failed. I love them, I say. I could have been the world's greatest animal tamer, you know. I have a rapport with wild creatures. I can sense their thoughts, their feelings, and meet them on their own level.

There is no animal I could not manage, no bestial level upon which I couldn't meet them. If I chose to befriend a beast, instead of killing it —' His voice softened, he looked off into the distance, across the darkening hills of an endless wilderness. He did not look at Wetherby when he spoke again. Perhaps he was not speaking to Wetherby.

'But I like to kill,' he said. 'I think, perhaps, I might even like to be killed – in the proper fashion . . .'

Their guide returned, dragging the skin behind him on a travois, and they talked no more of such things. That was the last time they hunted together.

Wetherby felt a vague uneasiness, recalling these strange words from that faraway place. Byron had often made him uneasy, in some indefinite way, in much the same way that he felt uneasy about an animal that was acting peculiar – when he couldn't tell if it intended to charge or to flee. There were many traits of the animal in Byron, at that. A strange man. Wetherby wondered if he had changed at all with the years, and looked forward to seeing him again. And that reminded him that it was late, and that he must rise early. He had arranged to meet Bell at eight o'clock in the morning, and didn't want to oversleep. Wetherby refused to have a telephone or an alarm clock, and depended on a method he had developed of setting his mind to awake at a given hour, but it had been some time since he had been forced to use this ability. He wasn't sure if it would still be effective; he decided that he had better go to bed.

Wetherby stood up and finished his nightcap, regarding the glowing embers. The door knocker clanked disturbingly through the quiet rooms.

Wetherby frowned, looking at the clock. It was a strange hour for visitors, and he didn't welcome unexpected visits at any hour. Then he shrugged, went into the hall and walked down to the door.

Bell stood on the threshold, looking flustered.

'Sorry to disturb you,' he said.

'Quite all right. Come in.'

Bell entered, holding his hat in both hands. He seemed

uncertain, preoccupied, no longer the same man who had recently
been with Wetherby at the club.

'Was there something you forgot to tell me?'

Bell shook his head.

'Come on into the study. There's a fire there. Will you have
a drink?'

'I haven't time, John. I'll have to go down to Dartmoor immediately. I'd like you to come with me.'

'Tonight?' Wetherby said. He didn't relish the idea. 'Can't it
wait until morning? I can take a train down and meet you there.'

'I want you to have a look at the tracks while they're still
fresh.'

Wetherby blinked.

'What?' he asked.

Bell seemed to snap out of the mood that blanketed his
thoughts then. He looked sheepish.

'Sorry, John. I guess I'm not thinking. I didn't tell you.'

'Tell me what?' Wetherby asked.

'The killer, whatever it is, has killed again.'

5

The police driver was expert, the motor-car was fast, and the
roads were empty. Wetherby and Bell rode in the back seat.
Wetherby had brought one of his sporting rifles and wore an
old bush jacket. He felt a touch of the familiar old thrill at the
start of the hunt, although it was greatly modified by circumstance. It was more like going after a man-eating tiger than a
trophy. It was very much like going after a man-eater, in fact.
They didn't talk much. Bell looked weary, his hard red face
drawn and tense, chain-smoking cigarettes. It was a black
night. The lights of London were behind, and on Salisbury
Plain they ran into the storm that was sweeping the West
Country. The slippery road didn't seem to trouble the driver,
and they shot on through the rain without reducing the speed.
Dawn had just begun to pale the sky behind them when they
pulled into the parking lot at The Bridge Hotel.

The driver consulted a map with the quick efficiency of long practice, pulled out of the parking lot and turned on to a secondary road leading north. He had to go slower now. They ran through hedgerows and trees, flickering shadows in the headlights, and then they cornered into a blinding glare of white light.

The area was cordoned off and arc lamps had been rigged. The narrow lane was starkly flooded in the powerful cross-beams and uniformed policemen moved in the shadows of the trees on either side. Several police cars were drawn up along the shoulder of the road and Hammond's warning flasher was still blinking weakly against the greater light.

Detective Sergeant Thurlow came over and opened the door. His face was grim. He carried an electric torch and his shoes were thick with mud.

'I've left the body where it was,' he said.

'Identity?' Bell asked. He got out of the car. Wetherby got out the other side.

'Yes,' Thurlow said. 'Driver's licence and credit cards in the glove box. Man named Hammond. A salesman from London. Apparently he'd run out of petrol and went behind the car to set up a flasher.' He glanced at the winking light. It was a sad little effort, overwhelmed in the glare.

'Turn it off, for God's sake,' Bell said, irritably.

Someone snapped the flasher off.

'The killer came out from the trees there, and Hammond ran some fifty yards up the road before it got him,' Thurlow said. Bell looked up the road.

'He ran past his car, eh?'

Thurlow nodded.

'You'd think he would have tried to get back in the car and lock the door, wouldn't you?' Bell said, more to himself than anything else.

Thurlow nodded. 'The locks worked on all the doors,' he said. 'I considered that. I suppose he didn't have time to open the door, or was too frightened to think of it.'

Wetherby had come around the front of the police car. He

was carrying his rifle. Thurlow raised an eyebrow and Bell introduced them. They shook hands and Thurlow's palm was damp.

'Anything else?' Bell asked.

'The same things. Plenty of tracks. They look like the same ones. The same thing that got Randal.'

'Who found the body?'

'Young fellow bicycling home from his girl's house. He's waiting in my car. Must have come along just a few minutes after it happened. The body was still warm when I got here. Gave him one hell of a jolt.'

'He's lucky he didn't come a bit sooner,' Bell said. 'I'll speak to him later. Let's have a look at the body.'

They walked on past Hammond's car. Wetherby still carried the rifle. The body had been covered with a rubber sheet, and blood had seeped out at the sides in thick coils along the road. A young constable with a very white face stood to attention.

'Pull it down,' Bell said.

The constable squatted and pulled the sheet down. Wetherby winced. The body was horribly mangled, the belly was torn open and the intestines trailed out in twisted loops. Wetherby had seen death like this before, and his first thought was that it looked like the mauling of a leopard. The young constable stood up quickly and walked to the side of the road; he leaned over and made noises.

'Did you find the head?' Bell asked.

'No. It's gone,' Thurlow said.

No leopard did that, Wetherby thought.

'Well, John?' Bell asked.

Wetherby was kneeling on the wet earth, looking at the tracks. Farther into the trees a detective was taking plaster casts and another was photographing them. Behind them a group was fingerprinting the car inside and out and measuring distances and positions. They all worked with quick skill, and would miss nothing, if anything was there. Wetherby looked up, frowning. Bell's face was suddenly etched in the flash of the photographer's camera.

'I don't know. I have an idea I've seen tracks like these before. But damned if I can place them. They're almost like a gigantic weasel at this point, but notice how deep the claw marks are. And farther back they're different.'

'Different?' Bell asked sharply.

Wetherby nodded.

'You mean there may have been two animals? Different animals?'

'Perhaps. More likely, the tracks changed when the creature began to run. The different stride, you see.'

Bell nodded. Wetherby stood up, brushing at his knees.

'It was walking up to this point,' Wetherby said. He glanced back at the road. 'It walked to here, and then it ran after its prey. That's when the tracks change. But Justin – when it walked – it walked on two legs.'

And they were silent for some time.

'Can you trail it?' Bell asked.

They were standing back at his car. The rain was still slashing through the light and black clouds had become visible as the sky paled above them. Thurlow stood beside them, nervously looking from side to side.

'Maybe. In the morning, perhaps. I'll need daylight.'

Bell nodded.

'There's nothing more we can do here now, then. We may as well go back to The Bridge Hotel and wait for daylight. We can get an early start from there.'

'If only we knew what the hell we were looking for,' Thurlow said. 'A man or an animal?'

'Something that walks on two legs and runs on four,' Bell added. 'A man or an animal?'

'Or some combination of the two?' Thurlow said.

Bell looked at him and Thurlow shrugged sheepishly.

'You don't believe in such things?' Bell asked.

'No. Of course not.'

But he looked very strange.

It foreshadowed the dark fear to come.

*　　　*　　　*

6

Wetherby and Bell returned to The Bridge Hotel in the morning. The rain had stopped but the day was grim with fog. They went into the lounge and sat by the window, their shoes caked with mud and their faces dark with the stubble of beards. They were both tired. It had been a night long with futility. Wetherby had attempted to follow the killer's tracks in the early light, had followed the spoor easily enough for several hundred feet beyond the road, and then lost the trail. The trail had simply vanished abruptly, as though deliberately obliterated, with no period of transition. There was a spoor, and then there was no spoor. Bell had followed, silent and dependent in this aspect of the hunt, while Wetherby sought a continuation of the tracks farther on. They had walked in a wide circle around the point where the tracks ended, but had found nothing; repeated the circle farther back, thinking that the killer might have back-tracked and left the original trail on a tangent; followed a long arc on the opposite side of the lane from the visible trail, in case it had back-tracked all the way with the instinct of the cunning beast knowing it will be pursued. But there was no further trace. It walked like a man, and ran like a beast, and Wetherby's tired mind wondered if it also flew like a bird.

They had returned to the lane after that. A police car was waiting for them, the driver leaning on the wing smoking a cigarette. Hammond's body had been removed but the dark stain of his blood still marked the spot where he had died. Bell stopped by the car but Wetherby had one more check to make. He squatted in the muddy lane and, using his fountain pen as a makeshift ruler, measured the depth of the animal's tracks; he also measured Hammond's tracks and then his own. Bell stood scratching his head. Wetherby had moved from the lane and taken a fourth measurement at the point where the killer had been walking. His forehead had corrugated as he looked at the fountain pen and struggled with his conclusions, and then he had walked slowly back to the car and they had been driven to the hotel.

'Sorry, Justin.' Wetherby sat, looking out of the window. The fog was drifting in long streams across the moors, a few motor-cars passed on the road.

'You did your best, John. If any man could have followed the trail, it would have been you.'

Wetherby shrugged; he didn't deny it.

'What now?' he asked.

'I don't know. I'm worried, John. I'm having some dogs brought down, but I wouldn't count on them. You still have no opinion on what it might be?'

'Less than before. None of the facts fit together. The marks on the body, for instance. I should say they were the work of a cat. Particularly the disembowelment. Not something as power-ful as a lion or tiger. A powerful beast, mauling the body that way, would have crushed the bones, whereas these wounds were comparatively superficial ... the ribs weren't broken, even though the stomach was ripped out. More like the work of a leopard. Something fairly light and completely ferocious, tear-ing with sharp talons rather than crushing. But that doesn't tie in with the strength necessary to sever the neck so cleanly. That would take unbelievable force.'

Bell nodded, crossing his legs. A shard of mud dropped on to the carpet and he regarded it thoughtfully.

'And the tracks?' he asked.

'They're vaguely familiar to me, but damned if I can remem-ber where I saw them before.'

'There can't be many animals that walk on their hind legs and run on all fours,' Bell said.

'Possibly an ape of some sort ... a bear for a short distance, although it's not likely. But there's another thing about the prints that I find even more confusing. The way they change when this animal begins to run. They become more shallow. Naturally, with the animal's weight distributed on four feet, the tracks wouldn't be as deep, but the difference was much greater than it should have been. I measured the depth of the prints, using my own footprints to test the resistance of the soil, and using Hammond's prints to make sure the rain hadn't affected the quality of the ground to any great degree. The conclusion was rather startling.'

Bell waited, leaning on his elbow. A waiter looked in the door, then withdrew. They could hear voices at the desk as someone registered.

'When the creature was walking,' Wetherby said, 'it weighed somewhat more than I do. Presumably it was balanced on its hind legs, and the print it left was roughly the same in area as my own print, but it was deeper. I should say it weighed somewhere around fourteen stone ... the weight of a leopard, possibly, nothing larger. But when it ran, the prints were much more shallow than the double distribution of that weight can account for. They were no deeper than a smallish animal would have made. Something around forty pounds.'

Bell considered this without expression and said, 'What would account for that?'

'It seems as though this creature just skimmed over the ground ... as if it were a large bird, an ostrich perhaps, not actually flying but using its wings to take most of its weight from the ground. And if it also had the power of flight, this could account for the way the trail vanished.'

'A gigantic man-eating bird?' Bell said, rather louder than he'd intended.

Wetherby's smile was weary.

'No, that isn't possible. I was just toying with some of the conflicting facts. No bird runs on four legs and has five distinctly clawed toes.'

'Well then?'

'The only alternative seems to be that it was fairly bowling along ... running so fast that it just skimmed the surface of the ground. Incredible speed from a standing start.'

Bell's eyes flickered as he added another meagre grain to his knowledge of the killer.

'So we know it must be exceptionally fast,' he said.

'But that raises another paradox.'

'Oh?'

'The victim ... Hammond ... ran for some fifty yards ...'

'Fifty-three and some inches,' Bell said.

'Yes. And how could a man have run so far if his pursuer was so fast? It didn't overtake him immediately, it followed him at an apparently great speed, and yet it didn't catch him for some fifty yards. Probably six or seven seconds. And they must have been terrible seconds for Hammond.'

'It must have allowed him a head start ... toyed with him ... that would be like a cat, wouldn't it?'

'Possibly. I don't know what to think. It almost seems as though there were two different animals. A large, two-legged one and a smaller four-legged one. But there weren't two sets of tracks, only one set that changed form.'

There was a considerable silence, although Bell's mind was roaring with activity.

'An animal ... a creature ... a being that can change its form at will?' Bell asked the window. Or perhaps he asked the dark fog beyond. He was thinking of what Thurlow had hinted, and Wetherby knew what was in his mind. But that was too monstrous for serious consideration. Too preposterous for belief. At this stage ...

'There must be some explanation,' Wetherby said. 'Some fact eludes us or some simple point that we have failed to see, or to understand.'

'Of course,' Bell said.

He continued to stare at the fog.

The waiter looked in again. He was a nervous little man, over-awed by the presence of a law enforcement officer, and suffering the guilt that all totally innocent men feel when confronted by an agent of the superstructure – fearing law far more than crime.

Bell signalled to him and the waiter came over slowly.

'Sir?'

'Coffee,' Bell said.

'Right away, sir.'

'And bring me some paper.'

'Paper, sir?'

'Paper, for God's sake. Something to write on.'

'Yes, sir.'

The waiter retreated with squared shoulders.

'Obviously a man who has never broken a law,' Bell said, showing remarkable insight considering his trade. He smiled slightly, perfunctorily, a man who would not hesitate to bend the law to achieve justice.

'We know so little,' he said. 'So many various facts without a pattern. The only way to get a killer like this is to wait until a pattern is established, and that is obviously not a satisfying method. How many deaths must occur before it links up? Do beasts conform to a pattern, too, John?'

'Definitely. More than man, I'd say. In their fashion.'

'Will this killer conform?'

'Yes. If only in the territory and the time when it kills ... the frequency of its kills. But it doesn't devour its victims, so we can't very well anticipate it by a hunger cycle. It will be strictly a bloodlust cycle, and to form a pattern from that we must know what the killer is ... or wait, as you say, until it establishes its own pattern.'

Bell winced. The waiter returned with a tray, coffee and a pad of writing paper, placed the objects carefully on the table and stood at attention. Bell waved and he departed. Bell tore a sheet of paper from the pad and squared it before him.

'Both deaths occurred within a mile or so of each other,' he said. 'Maybe that narrows the field, maybe not.' He began marking the paper with a ball-point pen. 'If it's an animal, it must have a lair somewhere in this area ... a cave, a burrow, a tree ... some place it regards as home. All animals have a well-developed sense of territorial possession, I believe.' Wetherby nodded, but Bell was looking at the paper and talking to himself. His pen moved swiftly. He was sketching a crude map. Wetherby watched the lines take form and context, and saw that Bell had committed the terrain to memory. He made a dark cross against a vertical line and the tip of the pen lingered over it for a moment, then moved on to inscribe a second cross. He regarded it for a moment, nodded, and printed a few words on the map, nodded again and turned it around. He tapped his pen against the paper as Wetherby looked at it and saw, with his trained eye, that Bell had incorporated all the significant points, and that the rough map nicely outlined the area and placed the territory he had seen in context.

The highway ran diagonally across the paper in a gradual south-westerly arc from top right to bottom left and this line was divided by a stream twisting horizontally across the centre of the sheet. The stream passed under the highway, and the hotel – named for the bridge over the water – was at the junction. The hotel was south of the highway, and opposite another line, representing a secondary road, made a right angle to the north. Beside the stream, west of the hotel, was the cross where Randal had died, and on the secondary road north of the hotel was Hammond's cross. The hotel and the two morbid crosses formed a triangle.

Bell's pen moved between the crosses.

'You can see that there isn't much distance between the kills, cross-country,' he said.

'What is it, about two miles?'

'About that.'

'Where is Byron's house?'

'Byron's?'

'I'd like to have a word with him.'

Bell drew the paper back and added another line and a square. The line represented a narrow lane running west from the secondary road and Byron's house was at the end.

'The lane leaves the secondary road quite near where Hammond was killed,' Bell said. 'Runs through the hedgerows for a mile or so and ends at Byron's. His place was the manor house at one time, but that was before motor-cars and the lane is quite narrow.'

Wetherby was judging distances, thinking he might walk to Byron's. He realized that adding Byron's house to the three points of the triangle formed a rough square. But that meant nothing. Bell was marking the paper again, just doodling now; he added the ridge lined with tors that ran parallel between the stream and the lane. There are no great distances in England, and the confined area gave Wetherby an idea. He looked out of the window and raised his eyebrows.

'Any ideas?' Bell asked.

'Possibly. I think we might treat this the same way we'd treat a man-eating tiger. I've done that before. Instead of trying to track it or anticipate it, we might attract it.'

'Set a trap for it?'

Wetherby nodded.

'How?' Bell asked.

'We could stake out a goat or something, I suppose. But obviously it prefers human prey . . .'

'And obviously we can't stake out a man.'

'If we could leave the corpse where it was . . '

'This isn't India, John. You know I can't do that. There'd be hell to pay.'

'Of course. Suppose I were to wait myself. Not in one spot particularly, just wander around the moors and roads at night? It's a remote possibility, but not all that far-fetched. There can't be many people on the moors at night, and if the territory is limited, then the killer's opportunities are limited as well. If I made my presence obvious . . .'

Bell scowled.

'Make yourself a potential victim? I didn't bring you down here for that.'

'It's been done before.'

Bell shook his head, considering more than refusing. Wetherby, now that he had had the idea, was rather excited by the prospect. It had been a long time . . .

'I couldn't let you go alone,' Bell said.

'It would have to be alone, Justin. This is work for a solitary hunter, not a posse. Too many people would simply give it warning. And, of course, it's not a question of you giving permission. I have every right to walk on the moors at night. Nothing official. No repercussions at all.'

'Well, I can't stop you.'

'It might work, Justin. I think it's well worth a try.'

Bell was still scowling. He sipped his coffee.

'What can we lose?' Wetherby asked.

'Your head,' Bell told him.

They finished the coffee in silence.

'I might be able to persuade Byron to join me,' Wetherby said. He glanced at the map again. 'We've worked together on man-eaters. I'll go out to his place this afternoon. But I'd like to try, with or without Byron.'

'As I said, I can't stop you. Officially. You still have your gun permits?'

'Yes. It shouldn't be dangerous, really. We're letting the confusing aspects of this affect our thinking. Justin. It can certainly be no more dangerous than any big-game hunting. It's not a ghost, nothing uncanny, just a beast that has to be killed – something I've done often enough for pleasure. Just because this is England the facts have made greater impact on us, the contrast has fired our imagination. But if I keep away from the rocks and trees, keep well in the open where it can't surprise me, it should be safe enough. Both the victims were surprised and unarmed, and both had a chance to run for a considerable distance before it brought them down. But even if it is as fast as those tracks imply, I'll be ready for it. I won't be running.'

'You sound as if you like the idea.'

'Ah, the old thrill, eh?'

'Any help you want . . .'

'Unofficial?'

'I never impose limits,' Bell said.

Wetherby said, 'I'll let you know.'

'More coffee?' Bell asked.

He had seen the waiter's eye appear around the corner. The eye disappeared again and they heard whispering in the hallway. Bell scowled at the door.

'No, I think not. I'd like to get cleaned up now and then go over to Byron's.'

'I'll leave the car and driver at your disposal.'

'Want to come along?'

Bell shook his head. He had no desire to see Byron again; he had an irritating idea that Byron had been laughing at him when he had requested an opinion on his former visit. He wanted more coffee and looked fiercely towards the door, willing the waiter to appear. Another man appeared. Wetherby stood up and the man walked directly over to the table. He was a small fellow, prematurely bald with soft eyes and a disreputably rumpled jacket. He looked like a rookie reporter and had a note-book and pens in his breast pocket.

'Oh God, the Press,' Bell said.

The reporter stuck his hand out at Wetherby.

'Detective Superintendent Bell?' he asked.

'Do I look like a detective?' Wetherby said, in a tone of horror that was only half assumed.

'Aaron Rose,' the reporter said, and mentioned the name of his newspaper. It was a Sunday scandal sheet. He moved past Wetherby and pointed his handshake across the table. Bell looked up morosely.

'Detective Superintendent Bell?' Rose asked.

'Do I look like a detective?' Bell snarled.

Bell sounded like a detective. Wetherby moved smiling to-wards the door and reporter Aaron Rose stood scratching his scalp and considering the deception of appearances.

7

The driver knew where Byron's was. Wetherby sat beside him, filling his pipe, as they drove from the hotel parking lot and turned across the highway. It was the same way they had gone before, when they first went to the scene of the killing and later, in the daylight, when Wetherby had attempted to follow the trail. This time they didn't travel so far up the secondary road but turned off on a lane to the left. Wetherby remembered noticing the turning before. They ran along smoothly, following the winding lane through hedgerows and sudden glimpses of open, rolling land. It was still foggy. The fog hugged the open land and Wetherby regarded it thoughtfully; he imagined how the moors would be at night and thought that, despite what he had told Bell, a night alone on the moors might well prove more terrifying than any jungle. It was a question of the unexpected, the startling contrast between danger and the placid everyday reality of this mild country. But this realization only served to increase his eagerness, and he looked forward to the hunt as he would have in the past.

Half a mile down the lane they passed a public house, a little thatched building which the driver eyed with a thirsty eye. It was called, with a nice twist on the traditional, The King's Torso. But in the light of recent events, it was an ominous name.

'You won't have to wait for me at Byron's,' Wetherby said.

The driver looked delighted. They drove on and after another half-mile came to Byron's. Wetherby got out and the driver reversed into the drive and headed back down the lane, where The King's Torso waited. Wetherby stood for a moment, his pipe in his teeth, surveying the manor house of former years. It was impressive. The building was well back from the lane, a timeless structure of different centuries and different architectural styles, with gables and turrets and stone chimneys, grey and grim against the windswept moors. From the back came the steady thump of someone cutting wood. The sound stopped as Wetherby walked up the drive, and Byron came around the side of the house, an axe over his shoulder. He smiled and walked down to meet Wetherby.

'I thought you'd be around,' Byron said.

His grip was as firm as ever. Byron hadn't changed at all, he was as timeless as his home. He was tall and lean, an immensely powerful man with the long muscles of endurance defined without bulk. His face was weathered leather and his eyes were bright with life; his hair was clipped short and his clothing was ancient. He rested the axe against the ground and leaned on the handle.

'So Bell has persuaded you to join the witch hunt, eh?'

Wetherby smiled and shrugged.

'I rather thought you might. I'm pleased to see you haven't lost the urge to action.'

Byron's eyes moved up and down, and Wetherby had the uncomfortable thought that he was being critically inspected. He puffed on his pipe and stared back. Then Byron laughed and clapped a big hand on Wetherby's shoulder and they walked back up to the house.

'I'm surprised you declined the offer,' Wetherby said.

'Oh, I have other interests. I haven't stopped living yet, John. I'm planning a South American trip early next year, as a matter of fact. Interested?'

'No, I'm still retired.'

Byron shook his head. They went into the house and down a cold and impersonal hallway with an atmosphere like a National Trust castle. They turned into a huge room hung with trophies. A wood fire was burning fiercely and the comfortable leather chairs drew the light deeply below the polished surface. They sat by the fire. Wetherby noticed the Kodiak bear he had watched Byron bring down with a single shot from a gun which was far too light for the job. It was mounted upright in the corner, its gigantic head snarling some nine feet above the floor, and Wetherby felt again that awe of a man facing that monster with one bullet in a .30–06.

'Drink?' Byron asked.

'I'd like some coffee.'

'Grant!' Byron barked.

A man appeared at the doorway. His clothing was, if anything, more ancient than Byron's, his hands large and gnarled and his face etched with deep lines. He had a twisted leg.

'Bring some coffee,' Byron said.

The man nodded sullenly and moved off, his leg wheeling after him.

'My servant,' Byron said.

'I thought you disapproved of servants?'

Byron shook his head.

'No, I disapprove of servile men. Grant is a most inefficient servant, but he isn't servile. He used to be a Cornish tin miner, a man who has experienced life to the limits. Restricted within those limits, of course. I hired him because he almost beat me hand wrestling.'

'What?'

'You remember the game, surely?'

Byron raised his forearm, hand open and fingers extended upwards, and made a pressing motion across his chest. Wetherby nodded.

'Oh, that. Yes, I remember.'

'We had a contest once.'

'You beat me.'

'Yes. It's not a game I lose. But it took seven minutes by the stop watch before I put your arm down, and I gained a great respect for you, John. I put Grant down in five minutes, by the way. Can you still hold your own?'

Byron placed his elbow on the table; he looked expectant, almost hopeful. But Wetherby laughed and shook his head, and Byron sighed.

'You look fit enough.'

'I'm all right,' Wetherby said.

'A pity you've given up life.'

'Just moved on to a different life.'

'Oh, it's the same thing,' Byron said.

'You can't expect everyone to agree with your ideas.'

'Never mind. What of this man-killer? What do you think?'

'I don't really know. You've heard that it killed again last night?'

'Yes. I heard.'

'I came down from London with Bell just afterwards.'

'You saw the tracks?'

'Yes. They looked vaguely familiar.'

Byron leaned back in his chair.

'Couldn't you identify them?' he asked.

'No, I believe I've seen similar tracks before, but I couldn't place them.'

'You should have been able to, John. Ten years ago you would have.'

Wetherby didn't like that.

'Bell told me you didn't recognize the casts,' he said.

Byron smiled, started to speak and then shrugged.

'Well? Did you?'

'Oh, casts are a different thing,' he said. 'I dare say I would have recognized the tracks themselves.'

'But you couldn't be bothered.'

'Exactly.'

Wetherby wanted to say more. Instead he refilled his pipe.

It was hard to know just how much to say to Byron. Grant returned with the coffee on a silver tray, swaying from good leg to bad with a curiously rapid gait. He banged the tray down on the table. The coffee spilled into the saucers, hands accustomed to ravaging the earth were not suited to the more delicate tasks of a servant. He swivelled about and clumped out of the room without speaking.

'I'm sure you'll be able to track this animal, anyway, John,' Byron said. 'You won't have lost all your skill.'

'I didn't this morning.'

'Oh, you'll probably have another chance.'

Wetherby stared at him.

'Well, if an animal kills twice, it's a good bet it will kill again, eh? I'm just being practical.'

'You think it is an animal, then?'

'Undoubtedly.'

'I suppose so. But what animal could have severed the heads that way?'

'It should prove interesting, finding out.'

'Interesting? My God, Byron. Two men have been brutally killed. This isn't a pleasure trip.'

Byron sipped his coffee placidly.

'Hunting should always be a pleasure, John. You know that. If it's necessary, that should merely add to the pleasure. And if it's dangerous, all the better.'

'I am rather excited about it,' Wetherby admitted.

'And it could be dangerous,' Byron said.

'Well, it certainly has the ability to kill a man.'

'What gun are you using?'

'I have the Winchester with me.'

'Too much gun,' Byron said. He sighed and sipped his coffee. 'You've seen the tracks, it isn't a large animal. You always did tend to carry too much firepower. It makes a man careless about his shooting.'

'But it will stop it,' Wetherby said.

'Oh, it will do that. If efficiency is what you look for. And if you hit it, of course.'

'I'll hit it. I haven't lost everything.'

'That's good. How do you propose to find it?'

Byron sounded interested and Wetherby leaned forward, hoping to get his old companion enthused enough to join the hunt.

'I expect I'll apply the usual methods. Treat it as a hunt. Try to follow a fresh trail if it kills again. Or try to anticipate it . . . wait for it, let it find me.'

'On the moors at night?' Byron's eyes gleamed. 'That would be like the old days, John. Remember the man-eater of Sunda?'

Byron gestured at the wall. Wetherby turned. The tiger's head snarled viciously at them. Wetherby remembered, all right. They had left the half-devoured corpse of a Hindu villager and waited for the tiger to return to its kill. The man's widow had howled heart-rendingly at such a misuse of her late husband, but the headman had showed more sense, or less emotion, which amounted to the same thing.

'You waited in a tree, John,' Byron said.

'And you waited on the ground by the body. Yes, I remember it. It was a near thing for you.'

'You never did see the beauty of that . . . that the risk had to be positive to make it worthwhile, that the man-eater had to have his chance to live or die the same as I did.'

Wetherby looked at the tiger's head again. He remembered the sudden blur of orange and black through the jungle night, that quick rush of death that had carried the cat's dead body past its executioner. Byron had fired from a crouch and hurled himself to one side as the tiger, already dead, stormed past to collapse at the base of the tree where Wetherby waited, where Wetherby had no time to fire.

'That fellow had already killed over two hundred human beings, Byron. It wasn't – it shouldn't have been – a question of the thrill. Killing it was a worthwhile end no matter how we'd managed it.'

Byron was looking at the trophy, too.

'Do you really believe that the lives of two hundred primitive and ignorant savages are equal to the life of that magnificent killer? Yes, I expect you do. Don't you see that the life of the killer is invariably superior to the life of the victim?'

Wetherby stared, not quite sure how serious Byron was. Even in the old days, his curious attitudes had never extended this far.

'You had all the ability a man could need, John. If only you'd had the philosophy. You could have been as good as I was. You were as fast, you shot as well, your instincts were as fine. But you waited in a tree, John.' The scorn was evident. It might not have been intentional, but Byron could not keep it from his tone. 'I could no more have waited in safety than I could use a weapon so heavy that even a poor shot would bring the quarry down. That was where we differed, and where you failed.'

Wetherby was stung. He sat rigidly on the end of his chair.

'Wasn't I as good as you?' he asked.

'Oh, perhaps. In your way. That's not what I'm talking about, John. Not ability, not achievement. Understanding. A way of life. Did I tell you I'm writing a book?' He stood up. Wetherby followed him across the room. A battered old typewriter was surrounded by disordered paper on a table in the corner. Byron picked up several sheets and looked at them; put them down again. 'A book about my philosophy,' he said. 'I'd like you to read it some day. You might understand, then. But not until it's finished.'

He turned and looked out of the window. The land rolled away behind the house, mist and cloud merging in the distance.

'Or perhaps out there at night,' Byron said.

'What?'

'On the moors at night. Perhaps you might learn to understand then, John.'

'But you won't come with me?'

'This – this is more to my taste, I will say. You are doing the proper thing when you make yourself the bait. It appeals to me. If I thought you were still the man I once knew I might join you – I might give you this beast. But you're soft now, John. We aren't compatible.'

'I'm not soft,' Wetherby said.

'Oh? Well, perhaps not. Perhaps I have misjudged you. But I'm seldom wrong about man or beast.'

'I'll be going now,' Wetherby said.

'You're quite welcome to stay here.'

'I've already booked at the hotel.'

They walked back across the room. The bear loomed up above them, the tiger grimaced in its eternal snarl. But these things were dead.

'You're angry, John,' Byron said.

Wetherby shrugged.

'Perhaps I was wrong. If I was wrong, I'll join your hunt. Will you prove me wrong?'

'I can't prove anything,' Wetherby said.

'You can, you know.'

Byron sat. He placed his elbow on the table and smiled up at Wetherby.

'You lasted seven minutes once, John. Can you last seven now? Five? If you can hold me for one minute I'll join you?'

'This is childish.'

'Childish? Basic, possibly. But how then are we to judge our fellow men? Come, John.'

Stung to anger, Wetherby sat opposite Byron. He flexed his arm several times and placed his elbow on the table level with Byron's. They locked hands. Wetherby wanted very much to beat Byron at this game. It was no longer childish to him, he was taut with that need. Byron was still smiling. His hand felt rough and dry, and he was relaxed. They stared at each other across their hands.

'Are you ready, John?'

Wetherby nodded.

Byron placed his left hand on the table and looked at his wristwatch.

'Proceed,' he said.

Wetherby drew a deep breath and snapped into sudden pressure, using all his strength in the first surge, trying to gain an initial advantage. It was like pressing against a concrete slab. Byron's hand did not move, it did not quiver. His long bicep seemed hardly to tense, but his forearm was a bar of steel that would not bend. His smile was unchanged.

'Ten seconds,' he said. 'I'm waiting, John.'

Wetherby pressed with all the power he possessed. His arm leaped with the effort, his chest swelled as the pressure ran along his muscles. He knew his face was flushed and his hand began to falter. Byron hardly seemed aware of the energy summoned against him. He looked at his watch again, and then he applied his own strength. Wetherby's hand began to move back through a steady arc. He was powerless to resist. His forearm drew towards the level, his wrist bent back, he felt as though his bones were bending.

And then his arm was down.

'Fifty seconds,' Byron said.

Wetherby shook his hand. It was limp and lifeless. All his energy had seeped away, even his anger had gone.

'Yes, I am seldom wrong about a man,' Byron said. 'But good luck in your quest, John.'

Wetherby walked back along the narrow lane. His arm ached. The police car was parked outside The King's Torso, but he walked on past without taking much notice. He was preoccupied with a sense of failure, a self-doubt and a troubling idea that Byron had, after all, been right.

8

The wind billowed across the rolling moors, shredding the fog in its wake. Wetherby walked through ribbons of grey mist against a black night. He made no attempt at stealth. His pipe crackled as he drew on it and trailed smoke lighter than the fog, a warm companion on a cold night. He was wrapped in a heavy cloak and had a hip flask of brandy and an electric torch. The torch was unlighted, and his rifle was loaded, the safety catch under his thumb. He was following the course of the stream westward from the highway and south of the ridge. The tors were black against a dark sky and the water made a rippling background noise punctuated by the regular croaking of frogs along the bank. His rubber boots squelched in the soft mud and reeds bent beneath his stride. Wetherby was enjoying this solitary trek; he hadn't realized how much he had missed the tingle of danger and the sharp sense of readiness. In that much, at least, Byron had been right.

Wetherby had left the hotel as soon as it was dark. The lights were still on in the bar, traffic moved along the highway and cars pulled in and out of the parking lot. But as soon as he had left the road he was alone. It wasn't a case of distance, he hadn't come more than a mile along the bank of the stream, and yet the feeling of solitude was absolute. He could just as easily have been in the darkest heart of a forest. It was the feeling he wanted, the situation he had looked for. He planned to follow the stream to the point where Randal had been killed, and then cut back across country, over the ridge and the open land beyond, across the lane that led to Byron's and on to the secondary road somewhere near where Hammond had been killed. From there he could follow the secondary road back to the highway and the hotel. It wasn't any great distance and he had all night. It was, he decided, the likeliest way to find his quarry. Since he was offering himself as the hunted as well as the hunter, there was little sense in waiting in a static blind. Concealing himself would have defeated his purpose, and there was little chance of seeing anything moving on the moors unless it came to him.

Wetherby walked on at a regular pace, carefully avoiding the large rocks and occasional trees which might have offered concealment, both to expose himself and to limit the danger of a sudden, unexpected attack. He moved in a zig-zag pattern, alternately heading upwards towards the ridge and then back down towards the stream. When his pipe had burned out he whistled tunelessly for a while, the innocent sound of a man who expects nothing, who is unaware of danger. Presently he filled the pipe again, and lighted it with the match cupped in one hand so that it did not dazzle his eyes.

He was very near the spot where Randal's body had been found when he stopped and took some brandy from his flask. It seemed a peaceful place, the stream bubbling along beside him and the moon attempting to get through the clouds. It was hard to imagine sudden death here. But Wetherby didn't allow himself to be lulled into false security. He remembered the mangled body in the road as he turned up towards the ridge.

There were more rocks as he drew higher and he circled around the larger ones, knowing that whatever the thing was he hunted, it had to get at him to kill him, and as long as he could see it coming he would be all right. All he needed was a few yards in which to bring his gun on to it. He came to the crest and paused, outlined against the sky from all directions. He could see the headlights of a motor-car moving along the highway and the land was a black gulf between. Somewhere in that gulf, it might be waiting, and he hoped so. He walked on.

But he didn't find it.

Or, perhaps, it didn't find him.

The King's Torso was owned by a retired naval man named Bruce Newton. Bruce was a dapper fellow with a clipped moustache and brightly checked shirts who didn't much care if he had many customers. That was why he had retired to this little pub on the seldom-travelled lane between Byron's house and the secondary road. One of the few regulars at The King's Torso was a young man named Ronald Lake, who lived with his young and recent bride in a pleasant cottage on the moors, a brisk ten minutes' walk north from the lane. Lake always walked. He had no motor-car, and there was no road leading to his cottage anyway, so he had to walk even had he not wanted to. But Lake liked walking. He had renounced the conveniences of the modern world after a few years of hectic endeavour in London, and was fortunate enough to have a wife who agreed completely with his desire for simplicity, and was perfectly happy to lead an uncomplicated life. They were both very lazy in a fine fashion. Lake had a small private income which maintained them in an economic and sufficient manner and left their time free. Lake dabbled at painting. He wasn't a good painter and knew he wasn't and didn't really care. He might have preferred to be good, given the choice, but didn't think much about it; he simply enjoyed painting and had no aspirations to fame or art. His wife was content to spend her time reading *Wuthering Heights*. They were pleasant people without pretence. Bruce liked Lake. It was the sort of customer he had visualized when deciding to become a country publican, and Lake was in the habit of strolling down to the pub four or five nights a week for a pint or two of beer. He always bought Bruce a drink on the first round and Bruce always bought the second. If he stayed for a third they played darts for it. Quite frequently, Lake was the only customer in The King's Torso, and that suited them both very nicely.

Lake stood up and stretched.

He had been working on a still life with flowers and an aubergine, and his clothes were smudged with bright reds and yellows and purple. When he pushed a fallen lock of hair back from his forehead, he left a smear of colour on his brow. Lake didn't concern himself with such trifles. His wife was reading in an armchair by the fire, a pretty young woman who might be overweight in later years.

'Well, that's enough for tonight,' Lake said.

'Ummm.'

'I think maybe I'll toddle on down to Bruce's for half an hour, dear.'

'Ummm.'

'Want to come?'

'Oh, I think not. I'll just read for a while, darling. I'll wait up for you.' She smiled and turned back to her book. Lake looked admiringly at the clean line of her neck. He loved her very much and considered himself a very fortunate man; often he wished he were able to express his love more intensely, but he knew it wasn't necessary. He bent over and kissed her neck and she smiled without looking up.

'I'll be back soon, dear,' Lake said.

He pulled a corduroy jacket on and tied a woollen scarf around his neck as he went out. He closed the door behind him and heard the latch drop into place. There was no lock on the door – in keeping with a simple life. After all, they had no enemies and nothing of much value, and locks had no place in such a way of life.

Lake walked quite rapidly for one of such a lackadaisical nature, swinging his arms vigorously. He could see the lights of the pub ahead and, to his right and somewhat farther away, the lights of Byron's big house. He had never met Byron, and

thought without envy that it might be pleasant to live in such
a grand home. But it was only a fleeting idea. He came out on
the lane and walked on down to the pub. There were no customers. Bruce was leaning on the bar chewing a toothpick and a
cosy fire jumped in the grate.

'Didn't expect to see you tonight,' Bruce said.

'Oh?'

Bruce was filling a pint mug without asking.

'I thought you wouldn't be walking around at night with this
killer on the prowl.'

'Killer?' Lake asked. He scratched his head.

'Haven't you seen the papers?'

'Well, I never take the papers. Since I renounced the hurly-
burly of life I find no interest in the affairs of the world.'

'Yeah. Well this happened right near here. Two men have
been killed in the last few days. Did you know old Randal?'

'Randal? The odd old fellow? Sure, I've seen him around.'

'Well, he was the first victim.'

'Good Lord.'

'Then there was some salesman fella last night. Got done right
up the road.'

'A maniac?'

Bruce shrugged.

'They say it's some kind of animal. Must have escaped from a
zoo somewhere. I had a copper in here this afternoon, told me
all about it. Said he was driving some big-game hunter around,
someone they brought down from London. So I guess it's an
animal, all right.'

Lake glanced towards the window.

'So I wouldn't be all that keen on walking around after dark,'
Bruce said.

'Oh, I'll be all right.'

They each took a drink.

'I don't suppose I should leave Hazel home alone, though.
She doesn't know anything about this, if she heard something
prowling about outside she might go out to have a look.'

'That wouldn't do,' Bruce said.

'What sort of animal do they figure it is?'

'Well, this copper that was here wouldn't say. Claimed he

didn't know. But I figure they know all right, it's just that coppers never tell you anything. The way I see it, if they brought this geezer down from London, they must have a pretty fair idea what he's supposed to shoot. That figures, doesn't it?'

Lake nodded doubtfully. He was troubled, not so much by death itself, but by the concept that death could intrude on his peaceful existence. He finished his pint.

'Have one with me,' Bruce said.

'Well ... maybe I'd better get back home. Just in case. I wouldn't want Hazel to be frightened.'

'Yeah. You'd better be careful yourself. If I were you I'd move a bit lively across the moor. They say it tore old Randal to pieces.' Bruce nodded then, as an afterthought of less importance, said, 'The salesman bloke, too.'

Lake looked a trifle uneasy.

'Well, thanks for warning me,' he said. He moved to the door and hesitated. The night was dark and the idea of another pint attractive. But he couldn't very well leave Hazel alone. He waved to Bruce and went out. He walked down the lane more rapidly than usual, his shoulders hunched. The cold was very noticeable and he shivered, wishing that he had worn a warmer coat. He left the lane through a gap in the hedgerow and started across the familiar route to his cottage, following the contour of the land rather than a definite footpath. He noticed that the lights were out at the manor house and glanced at his wristwatch, squinting in the dark; he had only been gone twenty-five minutes. He told himself there was nothing to worry about and smiled at himself as he looked nervously over his shoulder. He wondered if Bruce had been pulling his leg. The idea of some man-killing animal stalking these civilized lands was absurd ... as absurd as the eerie feeling he had of being watched or followed. But he walked even faster, so that he was breathing quite heavily by the time he could see the lights from his cottage. Some of his tenseness left him then, and he slowed down for a moment, then frowned. He saw the little square of illumination from the window, but he saw another pillar of light beside it, a narrow ledge cast out on the ground which could only have come from the doorway. The door was ajar. He looked around quickly and stumbled as his pace increased once more.

The door was open a few inches and Lake was shivering as he walked into the geometric rectangle of light that dropped from the opening. He pushed the door before him and went in, then smiled. His fear had been ridiculous, the dark night had seized his imagination. Everything was as it had been when he left. He could see his wife's arm on the chair.

'I'm home, dear,' he said.

There was no reply.

Lake wandered towards his easel. The bright reds and yellows flooded his vision. There seemed to be too much red. Lake noticed that he had been more careless than usual with his paint, there were heavy red smears on the carpet and red paint was dripping from the bookcase. His face clouded. It looked as if he had absent-mindedly squirted the oil from the tube in all directions. There was even a long red smear across the back of Hazel's chair. That must have happened when he'd bent over to kiss her neck, Lake thought. He remembered standing in this same spot, looking at the line of his wife's neck and thinking how fortunate he was. He looked now, but he could not see her neck. Only the red smear. He hoped she had not leaned back and got the paint in her hair.

'Are you awake, dear?'

There was no reply.

'Bruce was telling me a rather disturbing thing . . .'

His wife was silent.

She must have fallen asleep, Lake thought. He moved towards her chair. He thought he'd better wipe that paint away before she straightened up and rubbed her head across it. It didn't seem the right colour, somehow. It was a darker red than he had been using on the canvas. He looked back towards the painting, wondering about that, and reached down to touch his wife on the shoulder. His hand was on her left shoulder and he was looking back at the canvas. The red seemed to be lighter there. He let his hand slide over to stroke Hazel's hair. It slid on to her right shoulder. There seemed to be a great deal of slippery oil paint all over her shoulders.

Lake turned, very slowly, and looked down into the chair . . .

Wetherby had the reflexes of the hunter.

He was crouched, the rifle levelled, before the sound regi-stered in his conscious brain. His finger caressed the trigger and his nerves vibrated with the jangling surge of adrenalin, the heart-stopping song of action. And then the magic of readiness was gone, and he cursed silently.

'Wetherby!' Thurlow called.

Thurlow's torch turned in an arc across the heather.

Wetherby pushed the safety catch back on and came out of his crouch. Thurlow jumped, startled, and Wetherby saw that the detective carried a shotgun in nervous hands.

'It's all right,' he called.

He advanced. Thurlow stood waiting. Wetherby had just descended from the line of tors and Thurlow had come from the lane.

'Here you are,' Thurlow said. He pointed the shotgun away.

'Damn! If the killer was around, you've certainly given him warning,' Wetherby said. 'I told Bell I didn't want any inter-ference.'

'Bell sent me to find you, sir.'

'Did you have to be so obvious?'

'Sorry if I startled you,' Thurlow said. He didn't sound apologetic.

'Apart from the fact I might have shot you, you've ruined any chance of finding this beast.'

'It's too late for stealth tonight.'

Wetherby started to reply, then paused. He looked at Thur-low's eyes and saw the truth adumbrated there.

'It's killed again,' he said. It wasn't a question, and Thurlow nodded, pointing back towards the lane.

'Just on the other side of the lane,' he said.

They headed back together.

The bright flash of bulbs whitened the little room; whitened the pale faces of the detectives who were dusting for prints, and

blackened the streams of blood. Lake sat in the corner, staring
at his red hands with the wide eyes of shock and horror. The
full reality had not yet pierced the defences of his sanity. Bell
said nothing. He pointed towards the chair and Wetherby
crossed the room and looked into it. He winced. He hadn't
expected it to be a woman. *Wuthering Heights* was in her lap,
one page half torn out, her lifeless hand drooped over the arm
of the chair and her legs were extended towards the dying fire.
Her shoulders met in a dark mass of gore. The chair was torn
with the marks of bloody claws.

'Well?' Bell asked.

Wetherby felt his vocal cords rebel as he started to speak.
He closed his eyes against the surge of nausea.

'An animal?' Bell asked.

'It has to be. An animal or some dark fiend from hell itself.'

'But how did it get in?'

Lake moaned.

'I closed the door,' he said.

'Get him out of here,' Bell said.

Thurlow moved towards Lake. Lake would not move. His
limbs were solid and would not bend.

'It was closed,' he said.

Wetherby looked at Bell. Bell grimaced. They moved back
behind the chair, but they could still see her hand hanging
over the arm; saw a heavy drop of blood move sluggishly down
her middle finger and dangle for a moment before it dropped
to the carpet. It made a remarkably wet sound as it merged with
the blood beneath. Thurlow and a constable were attempting
to get Lake to his feet.

'Whatever it was, it opened the door,' Bell said.

'Locked?'

'No. There isn't a lock. But it's on a latch, it has to be lifted
from the outside.' They moved to the door. A detective was
dusting the latch and they waited until he had finished. A
photographer flashed a photo of it. There was no blood on the
door. Wetherby squatted, judging the distance from the ground
to the latch.

'What creature that left those claw marks could have opened

a door?' Bell asked. It was obviously rhetorical. They stepped aside as Thurlow led Lake out. Lake was still looking at his hands.

'I thought it was paint,' he said.

He laughed suddenly, an abrupt burst of laughter followed by a hysterical giggling which choked into a sob. Thurlow guided him towards a police van which had come bumping across the moors. He got in willingly enough, sitting rigidly in the seat. The constable got in beside him and Thurlow came back.

'There's something here we don't understand,' he said.

'That's a goddamn brilliant statement,' Bell snapped.

'No, I don't mean that.' He looked at Bell, a searching glance, and Bell turned his eyes away. 'Something we may never know,' Thurlow said. 'Something beyond the comprehension of man, perhaps . . . I think I believe that, sir. Something of ancient legend and derided superstition is stalking these moors at night. If it were . . . anything . . . it wouldn't surprise me.'

'Shut up, Thurlow.'

Thurlow shook his head.

'I can't help what I feel, sir,' he said. 'You can't alter that.'

'You're tired. You aren't being rational.'

Thurlow shrugged. He clamped his mouth closed, but he looked at the chair, and then he looked at the latch on the door.

9

The body had been removed, the police experts had made a thorough search which revealed nothing, and Wetherby and Bell remained in the cottage. Wetherby didn't expect to find anything that had escaped the keen and practised eyes of the police, but he hoped he might possibly see something in a different light, place a new interpretation on something already noticed and passed over. But there was nothing. Not a single hair had the animal shed, which was surprising considering the ferocity of its attack. There were plenty of claw marks etched in blood, but only around and on the chair. No bloody trail led to the door. It seemed almost as if the killer had wiped his bloody talons clean on the carpet before slinking off.

'You don't recognize those marks?' Bell asked, without hope.

'No. This is more difficult than prints on the ground. They were long, sharp claws but it isn't possible to tell more than that. There may be some prints outside, though. Although, as you've undoubtedly noticed the blood trail doesn't return to the door. Unless this beast can leap a considerable distance from a standstill, or fly, it appears that it has quite deliberately covered its tracks.'

'Shall we look outside?'

'We can try, although I think we'll have a better chance in the morning.'

They moved to the door. The lights of a motor vehicle came bobbing towards them, rising and falling over the uncertain terrain. Wetherby crouched and inspected the ground beside the door in the beam of his torch. He found nothing. The ground was fairly firm, but some track should have been left. The vehicle drew nearer, the twin beams flashed on the cottage wall and stopped moving. A door closed and a confused, howling din arose. The headlights went out and a single torch beam moved towards the cottage, bringing the noise with it. Thurlow came over.

'The dogs are here, sir,' he said.

'I have ears,' Bell said.

'There's nothing here,' Wetherby said, standing up. The dogs were straining and baying on their leads and the handler had difficulty in restraining them. Bell snapped quick instructions to the handler. He didn't like using dogs, they had no part in his way of detection . . . an element from the past, before scientific methods, and he had summoned them as a last resort when science was baffled. But he didn't like it. There was nothing about this case that he liked.

'You'd better wait,' he said to Wetherby. 'If these brutes can pick up the scent I'd like you to come.'

'Of course.'

'If there is a scent, they'll find it,' the handler said, his loyalty stung by the reference to brutes.

'Well, get on with it then.'

The handler took the dogs into the cottage. Wetherby and Bell waited outside. A cold wind was dipping across the land, singing a background mood below the excited cries of the dogs. Both men were struck by a feeling of displacement, as if this scene were occurring in the past, was somehow not real, as if they stood apart and observed but had no part in it. Thurlow's face reflected his own thoughts, and he said nothing. The dogs came crowding en masse through the door, tugging against their leads and digging at the ground.

'There's a scent in there, all right,' the handler said. 'I can smell it myself.'

Wetherby nodded.

'You noticed it?' Bell asked.

'Vaguely. It must have been quite strong before the room was filled with cigarette smoke and sweating men. But it was still noticeable. Like the prints, it's somehow familiar to me but I just can't place it.'

'An animal smell?'

'Certainly not a human smell.'

'This killer must be some animal,' Bell said. 'Some frightfully clever animal that can open doors and cover its tracks behind it ... so clever that it leads us to believe it must be human, even. But why in hell does it kill? The other two ... it might have suddenly been disturbed by them, been frightened or attacked through instinct when they fled ... but this ... it came into this cottage. It opened the door and deliberately entered to kill. Purely for the love of killing, the desire to destroy. If it is an animal – and it seems it must be – we can forget about a pattern, of course. But there must be some motive; even animals act for some reason. But why? We can eliminate hunger, it doesn't eat its victims ...' Bell paused. His face twisted in a terrible grimace.

'Unless,' he said. 'Unless it eats only the heads.'

Somehow, for some reason which was strictly emotional and strictly human, it was a terrible concept.

The dogs set out in a determined fashion, as if they knew their

job and were proceeding to do it well. Ten minutes later they
were as baffled as their masters. They didn't seem to know
what was expected of them, what trail to follow. They tried
to branch off in various directions, snapping at each other in
their frustration. Wetherby took careful note of their actions.
He had worked with dogs before, and he understood them. He
knew that they were defeated before the dogs themselves knew
it. He remembered how the tracks had changed as they left the
road on the previous trail, and wondered if this was what was
throwing them off the scent somehow. It seemed unlikely, far
more unlikely than the changing tracks themselves. It was not
inconceivable that a beast would run on four feet and walk on
two, but the idea that it could also change its scent was a different matter. And yet the fact remained that the dogs could not
follow it over open ground. There was no water to hide the trail,
no tree into which it could have climbed, but the scent abruptly
halted a few hundred feet from the cottage door. The handler
was leading the dogs in a circle around the cottage in an attempt
to pick up a second trail, in case the killer had back-tracked, and
Wetherby looked up at the sky. It was preposterous to imagine a
creature with those other characteristics flying, and he didn't
believe it possible, but he looked upwards. He didn't know
what he expected to see moving across that dark sky, but all he
saw were clouds.

'Apparently it has obliterated its scent, somehow,' the handler
said. He looked annoyed. 'The dogs can't seem to follow it beyond this point.'

'Then get those howling fiends away from here,' Bell snapped.
And they were indeed howling, not in the excitement they had
showed upon arrival, but in a tone that showed their absolute
frustration, their tails lowered and their eyes baleful. They followed their handler back to the van willingly, whining now. The
door slammed after them.

'Want to try in the morning?' Bell asked.

'I'll try. But I wouldn't hope for much, Justin. If it can lose
a pack of trained dogs so easily —'

'Dogs!' he snorted.

'Don't underestimate the dogs,' Wetherby said. 'I would have thought they could follow it. Not very far, perhaps, but certainly until it had reached water or trees, some means of breaking the scent.'

'I honestly don't know what else to do,' Bell said. He gestured with open palms upwards. 'Maybe this isn't a police matter at all, I don't know. Maybe I should put you in charge. Our methods don't seem very effective. How do you apply modern detection against something that kills without motive? Without a common denominator among the victims? Even with a madman, some pattern emerges. We could catch Jack the Ripper if he were still around, his murders had a pattern. His victims were prostitutes. But this thing . . . it doesn't kill whores, or poachers or salesmen or housewives. It merely kills. It seems to leave an abundance of evidence at the scene, but no way to follow it or deduce where it has gone. What in hell do I do, John?'

Wetherby didn't know.

10

They returned in the morning, dull with the anticipation of futility. The driver pulled over to the edge of the lane just beyond The King's Torso. They couldn't quite see the cottage from there because the land rolled up between. Bell told the driver to stay with the car and they got out. The driver lighted a cigarette and settled for the wait. A man came down the lane, wearing a belted trenchcoat and a felt hat and walking with a bouncy step. He had been standing outside The King's Torso, waiting for them. Bell scowled. It was Aaron Rose, the reporter, looking exceptionally eager as he approached. Another man followed behind him with a camera slung over his shoulder.

'Any comments for the Press?' he asked.

'None.'

'Can you predict when you'll be making an arrest?'

He had his notebook out.

'How in hell can I? I don't even know what we're going to arrest, let alone when.'

'May I quote that?'

'For Christ's sake no.'

'You didn't make any comments to the reporters back at the hotel, did you?' Rose asked, suddenly afraid that he'd blundered by anticipation, by arriving here ahead of the police.

Bell didn't answer. He moved towards the break in the hedgerow and Wetherby followed.

'Mind if I tag along?' Rose asked.

'Yes,' Bell said, with neither sarcasm nor anger.

'Oh. Well, is it all right to take some pictures at the cottage? The constable there wouldn't let us in earlier.'

'Yes, I do mind. Especially for that rag you work for.'

Rose winced at such reference to the Press.

'Listen, you wait here. Perhaps I'll have a statement when I get back. All right?'

'Yeah. Sure.'

Rose watched the two men walk away. The photographer fingered his camera eagerly. All he had photographed so far was the exterior of the cottage, and he was feeling slighted. But Rose suddenly blinked; his expression changed. He had just realized what line his story should take. Murders were one a hundred, man-killing beasts a novelty but not unheard of. What he needed was a completely different approach, a means of capitalizing on the shock and horror of human torment in the greatest possible manner. This was Rose's first big assignment and he desperately wanted to make it a success for sensational journalism.

'I think I've got it,' he said.

'Huh?'

'The angle. I think I have an idea.'

The photographer grunted. He resented ideas. They could not be captured on film. Rose began to walk slowly back towards the pub, his mind leaping violently. He didn't for a moment believe what he intended to write, but that was of no importance whatsoever. Few of the readers would believe it, either. But they would see the startling headline, and they would buy the paper, and Aaron Rose would be a success. He was impatient to begin his story, and annoyed that he knew so little background material; he wished he were in London so he could go to the library and gather knowledge of lycanthropy, to add a touch of learning as a sober background for the sensational headline. He visualized how that headline would look in print . . . how it would scream from the front page.

Does a werwolf stalk the moors?

Surprisingly, there were tracks.

The ground was firm, and Wetherby had not expected to find tracks, but they were there and they were obvious, deep and plain. They came from the house, but did not begin at the house. The ground hadn't changed, it was as firm as it was by the door, but the tracks began some distance away and continued in a straight line heading roughly north, and then they stopped. They went in the same direction that the dogs had attempted to follow the scent, and they began just about where the dogs had lost the scent. It was as if the trail had been deliberately left at this point, or deliberately erased on both sides, and the inconsistency was baffling. A creature able to move without trace wouldn't have blundered at random points, unless it was a deliberate attempt to lead its pursuers in a false direction. But then it seemed that the trail would have been left from the cottage itself, not beginning at a point some hundred yards beyond.

'It walked here,' Wetherby said.

'On two legs?'

Wetherby nodded.

Bell looked back towards the cottage. A uniformed policeman stood by the door.

'Nothing could have jumped this far,' he said.

'Nothing we know about.'

'Could it have run to here, and only left the trail when it began to walk?'

Wetherby shrugged.

'I'm beginning to think this creature can do anything.'

'The dogs . . .'

Wetherby nodded grimly.

The dogs had followed the scent to the point where the tracks began. No farther. They had not followed where the tracks were obvious in the ground, where the scent, if it existed at all, should certainly have been. Even Bell understood that there were implications to that – implications that led to far-fetched and mind-staggering conclusions.

'But an animal – or a man – can't simply cease to leave a scent,' Bell said. 'Certainly not where it has left an obvious trail.'

'That's right. But if the dogs had followed a certain scent to this point – the scent that they had followed from the cottage, a strong and noticeable scent – and that specific scent suddenly changed —'

Wetherby paused, not sure what he wanted to say, knowing what he thought, but hesitating to voice it.

'When the creature began to walk on two legs –'

Bell was watching him closely.

'If some change occurred – if it was, in some way, no longer the same creature that had run on all fours —'

'It's possible,' Bell whispered. He hadn't meant to whisper.

'I know,' Wetherby said.

But there were the tracks, commencing where the scent had ceased – where the dogs had lost the trail of the creature that had killed at the cottage, and where that creature had begun to walk like a man . . .

Wetherby could find no further tracks in that general direction, and once more he attempted to pick up the trail by following a circle with the cottage as the centre. Bell walked behind him in silence. The first circle was completed without finding anything, and Wetherby suggested that they move farther from the cabin and make another attempt. They both realized that it was futile, but there was nothing else to do, and they felt a great need to be doing something. They walked north from the cabin for perhaps half a mile, then turned in an arc to the west, circling and keeping the cottage as equidistant as unaided judgement could manage. The circumference of this path was thus about three miles, and they moved slowly. Wetherby paused to inspect the ground from time to time, spreading the grass and heather and pushing with his finger to test the resistance. They left no tracks themselves, and found none. The circle passed within a few hundred yards of Byron's house, turned back towards the east and skirted the lane, went on behind The King's Torso as far as the trees that bordered the secondary road and then curved back towards the starting point. They arrived back where they had begun and had found nothing. The sky was darkening and there was a smell of impending rain. They stood and looked helplessly at one another, then headed back towards the lane without speaking.

This course brought them to the line of tracks once more.

'I expect I'd better send a team out here to take casts,' Bell said.

'Purely for routine,' Wetherby said. 'These tracks are the same as the others, the casts won't be different.'

'I've been thinking about what you said,' Bell said, looking towards the cottage. 'If – if such a change were possible, how would it account for these tracks being plain here and then abruptly stopping?'

Wetherby, too, had been thinking. They were not thoughts that he liked, conclusions that fitted the facts but were alien to all his beliefs ... more, they were alien to his disbeliefs. He pondered for a few moments before he spoke.

'Granting such a metamorphosis, which I don't ... it seems obvious. A creature, a beast running on all fours suddenly undergoes a transformation. It becomes a creature that walks on two legs. Such a change would certainly have the strongest possible side effects. Perhaps even unconsciousness. And then, after a while, the creature, the changed creature, would stagger off in a stupor, perhaps not remembering how he had come to this place or suffering unbelievable horror and remorse. It might stagger away for a short distance in this half-conscious state before it realized the possible consequences of what it had done in its previous form. That would be when it might begin to cover its tracks, through instinctive self-preservation. This is all idle conjecture, of course. It isn't possible ...'

'Not the remorse, anyway,' Bell said.

Wetherby looked at him. Granted the initial premise, that had seemed valid enough.

'If it felt remorse it would want to get as far away as possible and try to forget what it had been responsible for, wouldn't it?'

Wetherby nodded.

'It wouldn't take the head with it, as a gruesome reminder.'

'I guess not,' Wetherby said, and they continued back to the lane. They came through the hedgerow by the police car. The driver had his hat pulled down and was sleeping. He snored slightly.

'I need a drink,' Bell said.

Wetherby nodded. They walked past the car towards The King's Torso. They both needed a drink, although neither was thirsty.

Aaron Rose was suffering a conflict of conscience and ambition. He sat at the bar of The King's Torso with his notebook open beside his beer. The photographer sat beside him. He had his camera beside his beer, but had no conscience outside the frame of a lens. He drank quickly but Rose sipped at his beer and considered his plight. Not that he had any choice in the matter, there was no decision he had to make and no way he could influence the results. But Rose was a man who worried about everything, and at the moment he was worried because his hopes were divided. It was quite simple, really, although nothing is simple to a man who worries. As a man, a man with a conscience, Rose hoped that the killer would be captured or slain before he killed again. The last killing had particularly influenced him in this, because it seemed far worse than the others, there was something so tragic about a young woman dying helplessly and horribly in her own home. But, as a junior reporter on his first big assignment, he hoped that the killer would not be found before the weekend, so that his story would not be obsolete for the Sunday edition. The report of a capture would not be nearly as thrilling and sensational as the story of these terrible unsolved crimes, especially the story he inteneded to write. Even any hint that the police were on the trail of the killer would dampen the shock value, for that depended totally on the terror of the unknown. Rose had the proper instinct and knew what sold newspapers. But, because he was a worrier with a conscience, and despite the fact that he could affect the result in no way, Rose was suffering with his hopes, and because he was basically an honest man he admitted his hopes even to himself. He admitted that he hoped the killer would not be uncovered before the weekend, provided of course that it did not kill again. Of course. And his face twisted in anxiety as he realized that a further killing would greatly enhance the value of his story. That provided a new conflict, far more terrible than the first, and his face provided the battleground of his emotions.

Rose turned as the door opened. Wetherby and Bell went up to the bar and Bruce moved down to serve them.

'You cops?' he asked. He looked very sad.

'I am,' Bell said.

'I'm a reporter,' Rose said, and mentioned his paper.

'Any luck?' Bruce asked.

Bell said, 'I'll have a pint.'

'No luck, eh? Can't you follow this animal's tracks or something? I mean, you got to do something. You can't have something like this running around killing people, can you? Why aren't you out looking for clues or evidence or something?

Rose slid his notebook up the bar, sensing a local colour angle.

'We'll get it. In time,' Bell said.

'Time? And what about the meantime? You gonna let it kill more innocent people?'

'Don't you feel the police are doing enough?' Rose asked. 'As a local citizen, I mean?'

Bruce ignored him.

'Give me a beer, will you,' Bell said.

Bruce shrugged and began filling a pint. He said, 'Guess I didn't mean to snap at you, but Mrs Lake was a fine person. Her husband is a regular here. It was a terrible thing.' He shook his head and shoved the pint over the bar. 'Can't you get the Army down here or something? Organize a search? They'd find it all right.'

'I'll consider your advice,' Bell said.

'You ought to.'

'Brandy,' Wetherby said.

'Can I quote you? About the Army?'

'You can just shut up, for God's sake.'

'My readers have a right to know.'

'Readers? You think people read that rag you work for?

They just buy it for the pictures of naked women and the juicier divorce cases.'

Rose looked hurt.

'He's right, you know,' Bruce said.' That's the only reason I ever buy it.'

'Can I quote that?' Rose asked, then frowned and thought better of it. He leaned sullenly on the bar beside Bell. Bruce set Wetherby's brandy down and Wetherby took a long drink, discarding the ritual of smell and taste. It went down well. Some of the tenseness left him, the mental construction of fact without belief. He took a second swallow and the door opened. Byron came in.

'Saw the car down the road,' he said. He had a heavy walking stick and a tweed cap. He walked over to the bar and stood beside Wetherby. Bell turned slightly away.

'Are you pursuing your investigations here?' Byron asked.

Wetherby saw Bell tense. He said, 'I suppose you've heard about last night?'

Byron nodded. Bell doused his anger with beer.

'Any tracks?' Byron asked.

'Some. Not enough to follow.'

'No? That's a shame. I thought that by now your old skill might have returned.'

'No one could have followed that trail.' Wetherby said.

Byron smiled. He ordered a beer and leaned his stick against the bar. Bruce slid the beer over.

'You're welcome to try,' Bell said.

Byron shook his head.

'But you're the man who's always right, aren't you? Well, this is a challenge for you. Wetherby says that no man could follow that trail. What about it?'

'Oh, doubtless he's right,' Byron said, smiling again.

Bruce said, 'Didn't you used to be a big-game hunter, Mr Byron?'

'I am a hunter. Yes. You misuse the past tense, my man.'

'Can't you maybe find the killer?'

'I haven't tried.'

Bruce looked from Byron to Bell.

'If you cops didn't want all the glory for yourselves —'

Bell said, 'Mr Byron has declined to assist us. I asked him.'

Bruce looked at Byron again.

'It's no concern of mine,' Byron said.

'No concern – are you crazy? Don't you care that these people were killed?' He leaned on the bar, his thin face pointing at Byron. Byron placidly sipped his beer. 'Hazel Lake was killed last night,' Bruce said. 'Did you know her? She never harmed a soul, never did a bad thing in her life —'

'I expect she never did a thing. Full stop.'

Bruce blinked. He looked like an angry badger. Blood flushed darkly into his face. 'I don't want your custom,' he said. 'Drink up and get out of here.'

Byron paused, the mug half raised. He was balanced between anger and amusement. Confronted by a man who did not understand his concepts, Byron hovered between scorn and rage for a moment. And then he laughed.

'Ah, you are angry,' he said. He set the mug down on the bar. 'That's good. I like to see a man in anger, with the courage to speak ... courage in his beliefs, stupid as they may be. It is, at least, a living emotion.'

'If I come over this bar, these cops will have to pull me off you,' Bruce said. He was half Byron's size and he trembled with his sudden hatred.

'And what about you, Justin?' Byron asked. 'Are you feeling anything? Does any semblance of activity begin to surge sluggishly behind that policeman's face? Or is it a policeman's mind that vegetates there?'

'What in hell is wrong with you?' Wetherby asked.

'Wrong? Nothing. Perhaps I'm a trifle outspoken. But don't you see? If people feel anything, even anger, or fear, even doubt, then at least they are alive.' He stared at Wetherby for a moment. 'If you are alive enough, then you will find your killer,' he said.

Byron turned and walked out, tapping his stick along the floor. He didn't hurry. Bruce's eyes bulged after him, as though he wanted to send his eyeballs like bullets into Byron's back.

'That heartless bastard,' he muttered.

Rose was gaping.

'Who was that?' he asked.

No one answered him. Byron was gone, and he had left a vacuum of black silence behind him . . . a vacuum which only their own thoughts could fill, and they were not pleasant thoughts and they led towards unspeakable conclusions.

II

Fear stood over the land.

It was a blanket of fear, invisible but oppressive and intense, and it covered the moors like an overcast sky, more ominous than an impending storm. The fear was all the greater because the people did not know what it was they feared, what the monstrous being was that had three times struck so terribly. They no longer spoke of it often, as they had at first, for the fear had increased with each killing and reached absolute intensity with the death of Hazel Lake, peacefully reading by her fireside. This was a people who had long regarded their home as their castle, sanctuary inviolate, and a new dimension was added to their terror. Nowhere was safe, this fiend might come at any time, to any place, and anyone might be his next victim. It wasn't death itself that brought such consuming fear, it was the unknown quality of that death, the method of dying and the agony of wondering if the creature would strike again . . . where it would strike . . . whom it would kill. Superstition, never far below the surface of civilized minds, came bubbling up in globules of terror, bursting and enflaming the brain.

The national newspapers played up the horror, capitalizing on shock, and sensationalism sold papers throughout the rest of the country. But in those few square miles where the creature had struck, it was pure fear that sold papers, and trembling hands that held them opened to the headlines of horror. The majority of the papers played with the angle of doubt, the uncertainty whether it was man or beast, but Aaron Rose's scandal sheet pulled out all the stops on the lycanthrope line. The editor was immensely pleased with Rose's story, and ran a companion piece dealing with the supposedly recorded instances of werwolves, and ghouls in the Balkans and, killing two birds with one stone, hinted that the killer was obviously an immigrant or at least of foreign extraction, since Englishmen were never wer-wolves. The editorial questioned police efficiency in no uncertain terms, asking whether any attempt had been made to establish a lunar cycle and whether the amount of blood remaining in the corpses had been measured, on the chance that it might be a vampire. No one connected with the paper believed the story line, certainly, but that didn't matter at all.

Aaron Rose was not as pleased with his success as he might have been, however. He was closer to the killings and farther from the editorial offices, and he felt the fear surrounding him. He worried, thinking that his story might have added to that fear, but justified himself by thinking that it was just as well that the people were afraid, that it would make them more cautious. When he was not worrying, he was planning his next story, intending to focus it around local comment and opinion, but he found that more difficult than he had imagined. People who would normally have jumped at a chance to be quoted in a national newspaper looked at him solemnly and said nothing; they resented being asked to comment about something so overwhelming, so tragic and so close to home. It was far beyond the point of being a topic of conversation. Rose abandoned the direct approach and went into the nearest market town to mingle with the populace and overhear their private words. It was a small village on the moors with narrow cobbled streets and several cheerful-looking pubs, but when he entered the pubs the pervading sense of gloom was severe. Faces were pale in the gloomy interior and conversation was hushed and solemn. Rose settled himself in a dark corner and listened. He heard one bold fellow announce that this killer was a fiend and should be tor-tured to death, but heard several whisper the question that plagued them all: what is this thing that walks among us in the night? And when Aaron Rose looked into their eyes, he knew that everyone shared the common thought: who is next? Who is next? And Rose felt a sympathetic twinge of the freezing fear that closed its fetid talons on these people; he felt it reach out to grasp at his own heart ...

The police were helpless, and Justin Bell underwent agonies of indecision, not knowing whether to concentrate his search on man or beast, and beleaguered by dark concepts he hadn't known lurked in his mind – unspoken and vague primordial fears that had been carried through the aeons since man's ancestors crawled out of the slime and began their ascent. He told himself that it was an anamorphosis, a deformed figure which would appear in proportion if only he could view it correctly, but at the same time he feared it was something that could never be shaped by human logic, something beyond the understanding of man because it was more than man and less than man, some monstrous combination of man and beast from a dimension apart from ours. At times, in the light of day, he ridiculed himself for such fanciful thoughts, but in the night the facts came tumbling back – it walked as a man and ran as a beast, it possessed talons that could shred human flesh and still open doors, the strength to tear a man's head off and the grisly desire to carry that head away to its lair. It could change its tracks and alter its scent, and was transmogrification beyond such a being?

Bell began to place more and more faith in Wetherby, perhaps with a subconscious desire to relieve himself of some of the terrible burden of helplessness and absolve himself of some of the guilt if it killed again . . .

And Wetherby failed.

Each night he walked the windswept moors and each morning he returned tired and drawn with more than physical fatigue. It had ceased to be a pleasure. Alone in the night, his shoulder-blades drew together across the icy bridge of his backbone, and he had a constant and terrible sensation that he was being watched; that the creature followed him and waited for him; that it had the ability to differentiate between a helpless victim and a dangerous opponent, and was waiting for Wetherby to make the fatal slip, the sudden irrevocable blunder through lack of concentration or failure of awareness which would transform him from hunter to hunted, opponent to victim. At times this feeling of being watched was so powerful that Wetherby halted abruptly and spun about, crouched and ready, positive that the creature was behind him. But he saw nothing. At other moments, loathing his own fear, he would shout aloud as a challenge to the unseen beast and stand tense and strained, listening for an answer that did not come, listening to silence on those anechoic moors.

Wetherby was not a man of fear.

He had never taken deliberate chances as Byron did, but he had never declined a necessary risk. He had followed wounded lions into thick bush and faced charging buffalo with steady nerves, but this uncertainty ate at his courage, the sensation of being watched from the dark devoured his confidence, and he knew he would soon begin to make mistakes; knew he could afford no mistakes; began to believe that Byron had been right, that he had lost his skill and grown soft. It was necessary to force himself away from the warmth of the hotel as night fell, and he had no willing determination left – only the lever of pride to keep him at his quest. And when another night's vigil was over, he had to admit the relief he felt at returning to his comfortable bedroom once more . . . the desire to crawl into his bed and sleep which went far beyond physical tiredness.

But he did not sleep well.

He drew the blinds against the dawn and went to bed, but when sleep came it was disturbed. He dreamed. Confused images danced through his mind, snatches from the past mingled with some uncertain future, a jumbled connexion between the two binding them together. He saw the dream image of himself, felt the heaviness of his limbs and knew he could not move quickly; heard a howling wind and felt a cold solitude, and then there was a rush, sudden and blinding, and he moved very slowly to face it, his rifle stiff and unmanageable in his hands. The creature was upon him, he felt its foul breath flow over his face, felt fangs sink into his flesh and fiendish haunches draw up for the fatal stroke. He looked into the creature's face – and awoke, sweating and writhing in his bed, with only a nightmare hint of what the creature had been, only a half-remembered glimpse of a near-human countenance; and half-awake, Wetherby wondered where he could have a silver bullet moulded . . .

*　　*　　*

Wetherby was sitting in the hotel lounge with Aaron Rose when Byron walked in. Wetherby had become rather fond of Rose. He realized that the reporter had depths beyond ambition, and found him pleasant company when he was not inscribing the conversation in his notebook. Ambition was not the same thing to Wetherby as it was to Rose, because he had never needed success in the same fashion, but he could sympathize with it, and tolerate it. Rose noticed Byron first, and remembered him from that rather violent conversation at The King's Torso. Byron was memorable. Wetherby was surprised to see him there, and for some reason could not remember whether he was angry with Byron or not. It was some paradox of the emotions that Byron inspired in him.

'Good morning,' Byron said.

He smiled pleasantly. He was wearing shabby tweeds and had a fine pair of field-glasses slung over his shoulder. A metal badge hung from his lapel.

'I'm on my way to the races,' he said. 'Newton Abbot. Thought you might care to join me.'

For a moment, Wetherby was tempted to agree. He would have liked to get away from this place, to forget all about the killings and his fruitless hunt. But he knew that the thoughts would accompany him.

'No. Thanks for asking, but I don't much feel like it now.'

Byron pulled a chair up and sat down. Rose was watching him closely, with marked interest.

'You look worried, John.'

'Certainly I'm worried.'

'No results as yet, I take it?'

'No, nothing. I've been out there every night without a glimpse or a sound. Nothing at all. And yet I get the feeling that I've been very close to it many times. You know the sensation, Byron. The eerie feeling that I'm being watched. That it is waiting for me to blunder. The same way you feel when you're after a wounded buffalo and you know damn well that it has doubled back and is waiting beside the trail.'

'Yes, I know the feeling,' Byron said. He made it sound like a great pleasure, a sensation in which he took delight.

'If only I could be sure . . .'

'Sure? Sure of what?'

'If I knew for certain it was waiting for me, it would be better. I would be calmer. But I can't tell, I don't know if my sense is reliable or if my mind is playing tricks.'

'Ah, John. You may lose your reflexes but you never lose your intuition. If you feel it is there, it is there. Uncertainty is a civilized trait, don't let self-doubt take command. When you stalked a wounded buffalo, you had no doubts. You knew it was waiting. You didn't know when it would come, or where it would come from, but you knew positively that it would come. And it did. You didn't have much time, John. A buffalo comes with its head lowered and the boss protecting its head and you had to shoot fast and well the first time. You did, of course, because you are sitting here alive. But in those days you knew it was coming. And now you tell me that you can't be sure, that you can't trust your sensations?' He looked into Wetherby's eyes and cold fingers walked up Wetherby's vertebrae.

'You've lost it all, John,' he said, softly. 'When this thing wants you, it will take you. It will wait and you will be too slow and it will take you. When it wants.'

Wetherby and Byron looked at each other, and Rose looked from one to the other with his mouth open. Then Wetherby lowered his eyes. A thought that he didn't like at all had stirred in his mind.

'Perhaps,' he said.

They didn't speak for a while. Then Byron, his tone matter-of-fact now, said: 'The trouble is that you are too involved, John. You feel too strongly, your mind has centred upon what this creature has done, rather than what you intend to do. This isn't a hunt, as far as you're concerned, you feel you must kill this thing before it strikes again. But, you know, these killings may not be a bad thing.'

Byron looked out the window.

'I've seen people alive with fear. Seen farmers carrying guns on their way to the barn, housewives looking over their shoulders in crowded streets. They are alert, they are alive because the possibility of death hangs over their minds.'

'And that isn't a bad thing?'

'I think not. When is a man more alive than on his way to the gallows? What cigarette tastes as good as the last one, when the firing squad is waiting? These deaths may well turn out to be a benefit, in the end. When they can be viewed with proper distance and objectivity. A few useless lives snuffed out, and ten thousand people granted the awareness of their existence, the joy of their survival.'

'You can't believe that, Byron,' Wetherby said, but he knew that Byron did.

Byron shrugged.

'Oh, it's one point of view,' he said. 'Are you sure you won't come with me? Steeplechasing. A dangerous game and a fine sport. A National Hunt jockey has an awareness of life which is arcane in our jaded society. I would have liked to be a steeplechase jockey. Ride in the Grand National. Think of the fullness of feeling as Becher's looms up before you and horses are thundering on all sides . . .' Byron's mind had wandered, he shifted in his chair as though in a saddle, then returned to reality and laughed at his daydream.

'No, I won't go,' Wetherby said.

Byron shrugged. Bell appeared at the doorway, saw Byron and screwed his face up in distaste as he crossed the room. Byron stood up.

'Well, I'll be off then,' he said.

He moved away, passing Bell. They didn't speak.

'Is he mad?' Rose asked.

'I often wonder.'

'There's something about his voice – his tone of voice – when he speaks of danger of death. I wonder . . .'

Bell sat down. He showed distaste for Rose, too, but not as greatly as he had for Byron.

'Any news?' Rose asked.

'I've decided to request a massive search by the Army,' Bell said. He spoke to Wetherby, but Rose got his notebook out.

'And what will they be told to look for?' Wetherby asked.

'God knows,' Bell said.

Rose wrote it down faithfully.

12

Wetherby had followed the same pattern in his nightly searches, following the stream at first and then cutting back over the ridge and across the lane towards the secondary road. He saw no reason to expand this area, since it encompassed the three places where the killer had struck, but he decided to vary it by starting from the other direction. He had no hopes that this would bring results, but it was at least a variation and might make him feel less helpless and, too, if the creature had indeed been watching him he might well surprise it by approaching from the opposite direction. But he had few hopes of this, either; he felt that the creature knew exactly where he was at all times, and would make no mistakes – an eerie certainty that he would never encounter it until the creature wished him to. Wetherby hated these thoughts, for they seemed to sum up all the failure of nerve and instinct that Byron had accused him of, but they dogged his mind relentlessly, ready to pounce the moment his conscious will relaxed for a moment, clinging despite his efforts to shake them away.

Wetherby was feeling the strain of his vigil.

He came out of the hotel at dusk. It was a pleasant evening, remarkably warm and cloudless and the moors rolled away in a patchwork of moonlight. Wetherby rather wished that he had gone to the races with Byron, that he had nothing more important on his mind than to study a form book and search for a decent-priced winner. He waited at the verge of the highway for a motor-car to pass, and Aaron Rose came running after him.

'Mind if I walk along with you for a ways?'
'Of course.'
They crossed the highway and headed up the secondary road.
'That's a nice-looking weapon,' Rose said.
'It will do the job. If I ever get a chance to use it.'
'You sound discouraged.'

Wetherby shrugged.

'Listen, any chance I could come with you tonight?'

'Absolutely none.'

'I'm not frightened.'

'It isn't that,' Wetherby said. He was almost tempted to grant the request. It would have been much easier if he had a companion. But he knew that would defeat his purpose; that the beast would never show if he were not alone, and that he would be sacrificing whatever chance he had to his failure of nerve, his growing dread of being alone. He said, 'I don't want to be responsible for anyone else, and this creature would be wary if I weren't alone.'

'Yeah. I guess. I admire you, going after it alone. It takes courage, Wetherby. I'd like to do an article about it. Later, of course. When it's over.'

Wetherby smiled faintly. They had come to the turning on to the lane, and followed it along between the hedgerows. An old man on a bicycle pedalled past, going home earlier than usual from the pub. No one stayed out late now. They walked on in silence until they were at The King's Torso.

'Want a drink before you start?' Rose asked.

Wetherby looked at the sky. There was still some light low in the east – as good an excuse as any for delaying.

'All right,' he said.

There was only customer in the pub – Grant the ex-miner, sitting in the corner with a pint of beer. He didn't look at them as they entered, his eyes were turned to the past, towards the bowels of the earth. Rose had a whisky and Wetherby drank a brandy. It tasted good, and he wanted another, but he knew that would not be wise. There was no light left in the east and he set out with forced determination.

'Good man, that,' Rose said.

'Hasn't done Hazel Lake much good,' Bruce said.

'Who has? He's trying.'

'Yeah, I guess that's right. If I had a gun, I'd get out after it myself. Don't have a gun. Read your story in the paper on Sunday. Load of old rubbish, you ask me.'

Rose didn't argue.

'Werwolves! Ain't no werwolves. Leastwise, not in England. Might be an immigrant, though, you can't never tell. Or some animal that was sneaked in to avoid quarantine.'

Grant looked up. His eyes were deep set in curiously hollow sockets, as if he had come to resemble the holes he had gouged in the earth.

'It's no animal,' he said.

His voice was hollow, too, as though he carried his own echoes in his throat.

'What do you think it is, then? Bruce asked.

'They're making a mistake, looking for it above the ground. That's all I'll say.'

'You think it lives in a cave?' Rose asked, looking for an angle.

'Not a cave. In the earth. None of you ever been down in the earth. You don't know. No one knows, if he's never been down in the earth. There are strange things there.'

'Like what?' Rose asked.

Grant looked at his empty mug.

'Will you have a drink with me?'

Grant nodded sullenly, taking no favours. He came up to the bar. Bruce filled his mug.

'You were saying?' Rose prompted, jotting the price of a pint on his expense account.

'Eh?'

'These subterranean creatures?'

'Oh, aye. Strange things. You can hear them moving in the shafts and tunnels. And in the rocks, too. They know how to move along the veins. Strange, slimy creatures, oozing through the earth. And stink! You can smell 'em for days after they've been in a tunnel.'

'Have you ever seen one?'

'Not me. Once a man's seen one . . . they got him!'

He grasped Rose's jacket suddenly, pulling his face close and hissing the final words. Rose leaped in his strong hands.

'Once they got a man in their slimy claws, you never see him again. They suck him back into the rocks. Just like that. Slurp and he's gone. They hate men, because men have come down to their home, you see. Men disturb them with explosions and drills, and they get even by causing cave-ins. We wake them up, tunnelling through their level, and they don't like it. Oh, we know all about them. We know.'

'Why haven't the miners told anyone about these things?'

'We have. But it's all hushed up, you see. The mine owners won't let it get out. They're all in league with the politicians. If people knew what lurks down there, well pretty soon no one would become a miner, see. They're bloody clever, those mine owners. They don't give a damn how many men get slurped into the rock.'

Grant stared intensely at Rose. Rose wriggled free from his hands.

'You think this killer comes from under the ground, then?'

'Where else could it come from? Eh? Where else? It figures, don't it? We dig down there, and pretty soon they were bound to start coming up here. And there are thousands of 'em, too. Millions, maybe.'

'Are there any recorded instances?'

Grant smiled crookedly. He had said enough for one beer. He went back to his table without reply.

'You don't want to take no notice of him,' Bruce said. 'Crazy. Works for that mad bastard Byron, so I guess he's crazy, too. Contagious, maybe.'

'Byron is surely unbalanced.'

'Yeah. The bastard.'

Rose sipped his drink contemplatively, his narrow shoulders twitching. He contemplated a subterranean approach in his next article, looked absently towards the window and started. He had suddenly realized that it was dark, and it startled him. It was a considerable walk back to the hotel, and Rose was a man who had never taken a chance in his life, who worried about the statistical chance of being struck by meteors as much as he did motor-cars. He was amazed that his preoccupation, even with the pursuit of success, had left him in his position.

'I'd better be off now,' he said, sliding from the stool.

'Say, you on foot?' Bruce asked.

Rose nodded unhappily.

'Well, you better be careful.'

'Yeah. I'll hurry.'

'Don't do no good to be careful,' Grant said.

Rose looked at him nervously.

'You won't see it coming. That's 'cause it don't come at you on the ground, see. It can suddenly pop up right under your feet. That's the way they get you. Pop! Just like that. One minute you're all alone, the next it's got you. Slurp! And down into the ground you go. It's a horrible death.'

Rose shuddered as he went out.

Grant moved to the bar to get a refill.

'Say, are there really things like that under the ground?' Bruce asked, looking towards his beer cellar entrance.

'Don't be daft. A beer's a beer.'

Rose walked quickly down the lane. He kept his eyes forwards, resisting a temptation to peer back over his shoulder and even to glance suspiciously at the ground beneath his feet, and he told himself that his nervousness was absurd; that the likelihood of anything (a vague anything, he refused to make his dread concrete by giving it a name) happening to him was so remote that it was unimaginable. He worried, of course, but managed to limit his worry to the statistical averages that had always plagued him, as if he were worrying about being struck by a motor-car. The night seemed remarkably dark, although there was a bright moon and no clouds, and the moon cast shadows along the hedgerows and did not benefit failing nerves. Rose began to play a game, fixing his eyes on some point a little distance ahead and concentrating on it as it drew nearer, until he had passed it and then fixing on a new point, breaking the walk up by dividing it into a multitude of short walks. It preoccupied his mind and lessened the tension.

A huge shadow loomed up before him.

Rose gasped and jumped. The shadow jumped with him. He turned in terror, and let his breath out in relief as his heart began to beat once more. It had been his own shadow, thrown before him by the headlights of a silently approaching motor-car. He stepped aside to let the car pass, his heart still pounding, but already calming himself with the thought that there was certainly more danger from motor-cars on this unlighted lane than there could be from his nameless dread.

The motor-car drew past him very slowly. It was a police car. The driver looked closely at Rose, scrutinizing him with hard eyes, and Rose felt much better knowing that the police were patrolling the area. The car speeded up a bit, winked red brake lights as it came to the junction of the secondary road, then wheeled around the turning. Rose wondered why he hadn't asked for a lift; he supposed that he'd been too startled by that looming shadow to think properly. He began to walk again. He looked ahead, seeking his next point of division, and noticed the red phone box at the junction some hundred yards ahead. That was a convenient point and he stared at it. It seemed to be moving away from him as his eyes played games of their own in the moonlight. He began walking faster. And then, gradually, he realized that whatever was walking on the other side of the hedgerow was walking faster, keeping abreast of him. He had so carefully shut his mind against his fear that the knowledge didn't register as a whole, but seeped into his mind in disintegrated bits. The terror did not come until he had actually turned and looked at the hedgerow; stared as the hedge parted, and he looked into the grotesque face of death.

Rose ran.

He ran as fast as madness could propel him down the narrow lane. He had looked into the face of the killer, but it made no impression on his mind. His mind did not function, he did not feel anything as his instincts took possession of his functions. Perhaps the soundwaves of the feet that padded behind him reached his ears, but his ears sent no impression to his brain. His brain was screaming too loud to hear. He stumbled, but was running too fast to fall; came crashing up against the phone box and yanked the door open; hurled himself inside this cubicle sanctuary of society and pulled the door closed behind him. Something slammed against the closing door with violent fury. Rose was still controlled by his instincts, and they were the instincts of civilized man. He had already jammed his finger in the dial and lifted the receiver to call for impossible salvation, when the door sprang open behind him, and Aaron Rose was drawn down with his finger still hooked in the dial ...

Wetherby came to the top of the ridge beside a mound of rocks and stood there, looking down. The stream wound through the moonlight like the slimy track of a snail and the open land between was silver-filigreed by the slender shadows of the reeds. Wetherby stood very still and looked. If anything was moving down there, he would have seen its shadow beneath it. This was the first night that the moon had been his ally. But nothing moved, and he saw little sense in proceeding farther in that direction. He decided he would follow the crest of the ridge back to the secondary road, carefully circling each rocky mound ...

Wetherby jumped with realization.

For a moment he quivered, taut and tight, and then he relaxed, cursing his stupidity. He had made his first blunder. He had climbed the ridge and stood beside that high peak of stone, hardly noticing it. He had stood there for several minutes. If the killer had been lurking in those rocks, Wetherby would have died beside them. It was unbelievable carelessness, a mistake he would never have made in the past, a routine that had been second nature to him – until now.

Wetherby was sweating. He mopped his brow and drew his brandy flask out. Byron had been right, he knew, and the knowledge brought Wetherby as close as he had ever been to self-pity. The tension had got to him, and the blunders had begun. He took a large swallow and felt the heat of alcohol along his cold spine. He thought, deeply and objectively, weighing the possibilities and loathing the conclusions. Then he sighed. He knew that he should not be there, that his day was past and his skill was gone. If he continued, he was going to die, and Wetherby did not want to die.

Wetherby turned slowly and started walking back the way he had come. His shoulders felt heavy, he was tired. He was finished. He wondered how he would tell Bell ...

Wetherby came out on the lane just east of The King's Torso. The pub had closed, the lights were off. It was just as well, because Wetherby did not want to see anyone; he felt that

his failure was inscribed on his face, that any man could decipher
the runes of his defeat. He walked slowly down the lane, keeping
in the centre and looking to both sides. He intended to make no
more mistakes now, and thought how ironic it would be if he
were to die now that he had given up the quest. All he wanted
to do was to return to the warm safety of his room, return to
London in the morning and close his mind to recrimination.
But, to a man like Wetherby, a man like Wetherby had been, the
knowledge of this was a torment far greater than death, and his
emotions began to rebel against his mind.

Because he was watching the hedgerows with his eyes, and
because his senses were directed against his mind, Wetherby
did not notice the phone box until he was quite near to it – near
enough to see the heap inside, to see that the door was slightly
open. The door was open because a leg protruded from the booth.
The receiver dangled at the end of its cord. Wetherby opened
the door and looked in. A shaft of wind blew past him and the
receiver began to revolve very slowly, turning just where the
man's head should have been. Wetherby recognized the man's
blood-spattered clothing with a cold lack of feeling.

It would make a splendid headline for the newspaper which
had employed Aaron Rose.

Wetherby's hand had already stretched out to lift the receiver
and telephone for the police when the savage hatred sank a
shaft into his brain. It was hatred of himself. He stared at that
hand that was so willing to seek help, and he hated himself so
much that it was unbearable, that the hatred had to be transferred to save his mind. He stepped out of the booth and let the
door swing gently closed on Rose's leg, moved away from the
lane and looked at the ground. The tracks were there. He
followed them. He was not being cautious now. He was possessed,
and caution was there because it was part of his possession; not
because he was afraid, but because he must live to kill. He would
make no mistake this time. The hunter did not blunder when he
did not think.

The tracks ran beside the hedgerow, back the way Wetherby
had come. He wondered, without caring, if the creature had

been crouched there when he walked past. The trail was plain for some distance before it stopped. But Wetherby paused for only a moment at the end of the tracks. Then he moved on. There was a broken stalk of grass, a crumpled shard of moss, the faintest imprint of a foot. There were all the things that he knew now, as a certainty, but he had failed to see before. He scarcely bothered to look at them now. His course was direct, and he knew with cold precision exactly where he was going . . .

13

Byron was waiting.

He was waiting beside the house, but Wetherby did not come up the walk. He came from behind the woodshed and the moonlight was running up the barrel of his rifle. Byron stood up and smiled. His smile formed a curious pattern on his face; he looked in some strange way relieved.

'You came silently,' he said.

He carefully leaned his axe against the house.

'I thought you would never come,' he said.

Wetherby said nothing.

'The races were excellent. A pity you missed them. There was a pile-up at one fence. Two horses killed and a jockey fractured his collar-bone. One horse had a broken back and they let it suffer until they could erect a tent around it, so that the people wouldn't see them kill it. That says something for our world, eh?'

'Where is it, Byron?'

'What, John?'

'I don't know what it is. I want it. I'm absolutely cold, Byron, and I can kill you if I must.'

'That's good. You really should have recognized the tracks long ago, John. You should have followed it. I know, because I very carefully laid the trail. Did you follow it tonight, or did you guess?'

'I suppose I knew all the time,' Wetherby said. His gun was pointed at the ground but the safety catch was off. 'But tonight

I realized something – perhaps it was something you tried to tell me. It was like a magnet, drawing me here tonight.'

'No. It was a touch of your old skill. That's all. The hunter's instinct.' There was respect and genuine affection in his expression. 'Do you understand why I did it?'

'I know the purpose in your deranged mind.'

'You still think I'm insane? But clever, you must admit. And I succeeded in giving these rustic clods a reason to live. Perhaps more than they deserve.' Byron leaned against the house. His hand played over the axe handle. 'If they had been brave, I might have let them live. Perhaps not. But John, the fear! You should have seen the fear in their eyes . . .'

'Was Hazel Lake supposed to be brave?'

'Oh, what does it matter? Her death made it more terrible for the others, that was all.'

Wetherby's finger caressed the trigger. But he couldn't kill yet, it was not resolved. He did not know himself yet.

'What do you think it was?' Byron asked.

'Which?'

'Ah, you'd realized that much. That's good. I made the two-legged tracks, of course. A simple matter of borrowing the claws from several different trophies and fastening them to an old pair of boots. Quite simple, but clever. You were certainly taken in by it. Half bear, half lion. But have you forgotten seeing those other tracks?'

Wetherby was forgetting nothing now, because he was not consciously thinking.

'Wolverine?' he said.

'Excellent, John. Excellent. Remember when we studied those tracks together. Must have been ten years ago now. You mentioned that a wolverine could never be tamed, I believe. It wasn't easy. I was forced to breed one in captivity to get any semblance of control. But then, I always did have a rapport with wild animals. I didn't really tame it, of course. I reduced myself and met it on its own level. It knows I am necessary for its survival, and we hunt together as equals.'

'My God,' Wetherby said.

'It gets in the cage willingly enough now,' Byron said, 'It's a bit more difficult after the kill, but I manage. See how simple it was, really? How effective?' Byron's hand had closed on the axe handle. Wetherby ignored it.

'But now, the question, John ... what are you going to do?'

Byron was balanced, his knees bent. He was enjoying it immensely.

'You haven't a chance.' Wetherby said.

'That isn't what I mean. You know I am immune to fear. In that respect, perhaps I am mad. A pleasant madness. But I've longed for you to come, John. You were perhaps the only man alive who had a chance with me. A slight chance. I was so disappointed when I saw how you had changed. How easy you would be. Are you going to try to kill me, John? Or will you try to inform the police? How much is left of the man I knew?'

'I don't know,' Wetherby said. Then he said, 'Enough.'

'Come, I'll show you my bloodthirsty little friend,' Byron said, moving suddenly away from the wall. He left the axe where it was, and the quick movement did not cause any reaction in Wetherby. Byron walked past him, close, and Wetherby regarded the space between his shoulders where the bullet would kill. He followed Byron. Byron swung open the angled doors that led to the cellar and went down into the dark. Wetherby went in behind him. It was very dark and for a moment he couldn't see Byron. Then Byron turned the lights on. The wolverine snarled from its cage, its stink filled the close room. Thirty pounds of claws and fangs and pure hatred, it turned its terrible eyes on Wetherby. He stared at it, a small monster that could inspire terror in a grizzly bear or put a pack of wolves to flight. Byron stood beside the cage. He smiled again. Wetherby raised his eyes reluctantly from the hypnotic gaze of the beast and looked at Byron. He looked beyond Byron and felt his stomach turn.

There on the wall, very effectively mounted on oak plaques, three human heads looked with glass eyes across the room. The lips were drawn back in snarls. And hanging from the ceiling, supported by a hook through the scalp, swung a face that Wetherby knew, a man that Wetherby had liked. Aaron Rose's head turned through a slow revolution, until the countenance was full to Wetherby, the face twisted in unspeakable horror and gore dripping from the severed neck. A white glint of bone parted the flesh at the throat. Byron made a sweeping gesture of presentation.

'My trophies,' he said.

Then he was not smiling. He was crouched beside the cage, his hand on the lock. The wolverine reached out with curled claws, instinctively, then drew them back with slow reluctance as Byron's fingers scratched its bristling neck.

'Well?' Byron asked.

Wetherby did not move.

'He comes fast, John. There will be time for one shot, perhaps. But I come fast, too.'

'Not here,' Wetherby said.

Byron's brow arched.

Wetherby knew what he had to do. What he absolutely had to do, beyond right and wrong, beyond hatred and fear . . . beyond self-preservation, if need be.

Wetherby worked the lever. The shells spun from the chamber and clattered on the concrete floor. He counted the clicks. Byron too, was counting. Wetherby worked a bullet into the chamber and stopped ejecting.

'Two bullets, John?' Byron asked.

'Bring your friend.'

'Ah. Quite so. I judged you badly, John.'

Byron was still stroking the wolverine. It was impossible to stroke a wolverine, uncanny and inhuman. But Byron was more than a man. Or less than human. The wolverine rubbed against him, but its eyes were on Wetherby and its fiendish jaws dripped in anticipation.

'If I was wrong, John,' Byron said. 'If men are beyond salvation, I have at least saved you.' Again he smiled.

'Here?' he asked.

'No. Out there.'

'Much better.'

'I'll walk towards the tors.'

'Excellent.'

'Don't be long, Byron.'

'No. Of course not.'

Wetherby moved backwards to the stairs. Then he turned and went up with his back towards Byron. Byron nodded in approval.

'I'll see you soon,' Byron said.

Wetherby was afraid.

But it was a healthy fear. It was not the strained tension of the nights before, his senses were alive and tingling, his blood pounded but his muscles were calm. He was smiling in the dark at the crest of the ridge. Every detail of the land was impressed effortlessly on his mind. A solitary cloud was drifting towards the moon, slipping through the sky. It was going to bring black night when it blocked that moonlight, and Wetherby welcomed the shadows because he had no need for light. He wanted very much to live, and he understood Byron at last. In that much, at least, Byron had known. He wanted to live because he was alive, and because the wind was blowing across the moors, and because he had two bullets in his rifle . . .

The Instant Divorce

David Learmont Aitken

Her lips were cold, her breasts were bare,
And diamonds sparkled in her hair.
She paced the floor and thought aloud;
Eternal love to him she'd vowed;
Now he was dead, and she was free,
She strode about, on fire with glee.
And then he moaned, and she stood still;
Her brain was numb, her heart was chill.
She whirled around, and rushed upstairs,
Her mad tongue mouthing silent prayers;
This time make sure, she told herself,
And took an axe down from the shelf.
He lay there writhing on the bed
As she bent down, removed his head.

In Mother's Loving Memory

Barry Martin

May 28th

The events of today have been very rewarding. Today I committed my first murder. I am very proud of the fact. It's not everybody that can boast about such a thing.

I was very surprised, on thinking about it afterwards, how relatively easy it was. You wouldn't think that murder could be so easy, but it is – as easy as anything. Anyone can do it if they make up their mind to.

I made up my mind as soon as I got up this morning and I just couldn't wait for this evening when I could go out and select my victim. That was the only bit I didn't like. The only really nasty part of it – selecting my victim. Having to go over to her on the street corner and make out that I wanted to do 'that sort of thing'. I really felt awful. I felt like spewing up in disgust.

Mother always said that I should never have anything to do with 'that type of girl'. Mother said that all girls, especially that sort, were wicked and sinful. So now I have destroyed something wicked and sinful. I know Mother would have been proud of me for what I have done.

You could see how evil she was just by looking at her. Standing on the corner, her hands on her hips, fluttering her eyelashes. Evil just oozed out of her.

Her flat was just like herself – dirty and cheap. An absolute haven of filth! I had to watch while she undressed. Watch her take everything off, one by one – skirt, blouse, bra, panties – until she stood before me displaying her horrible naked body.

I tried to avert my eyes, but I couldn't. I had to look. She made me look with her lustful wickedness. So, I picked up one of her nylon stockings and, before she could scream or try to stop me, I wound it around her neck.

I felt a sense of extreme satisfaction as I heard her choke and splutter, as I pulled the stocking tighter and tighter. Her eyes bulged and her face became quite bloated. Her tongue lolled out between her teeth and little drops of saliva dribbled down her chin.

Now she will never be able to ply her filthy trade again – the dirty, stinking, piss-sodden whore!

May 29th

I awoke this morning after a good night's sleep. The events of last night seem to have relaxed me somewhat – relieved the tension that I have felt building up over the past few weeks. After my second murder tonight I felt even better.

I found her in a pub. I was sitting at one of the corner tables, when I noticed her sitting at the bar. She was wearing a bright red coat with a black fur collar, her peroxide-blonde hair piled high upon her head.

She turned and saw me looking at her. I winked at her and took out my wallet. She took to the bait at once and fell straight into my little trap. She slid off the bar stool, walked over and sat down beside me. She sat so close that I shuddered. If she had touched me I don't know what I would have done!

She suggested that we should go back to her place. A hot flush of excitement came over me, knowing what I would have to do when we got there. What I would have to do in memory of Mother, so that she will know that I took notice of what she said.

She didn't switch on the main light in her bedroom, but, instead, lit a candle that was standing on the dressing table. She said that I looked nervous and that I would feel more relaxed if we did it by candlelight. What bullshit! As if she could think that I really wanted to do 'that' anyway!

I said that I was thirsty and went out into the kitchen for a glass of water. A tin opener lay upon the table. I picked it up, put it behind my back and walked slowly back into the bedroom.

She was lying on the bed naked and exposed, her thighs apart, rubbing her hands across her belly and smiling at me. The candlelight cast flickering shadows on her filthy body and she didn't see the tin opener until I raised it high and plunged it into her stomach.

Killing somebody with a tin opener isn't very easy. I had to keep hacking and cutting, and she wouldn't keep still and she would keep screaming. I had to work a bit faster to stop her.

I held the candle in my left hand so that I could see what I was doing. Little drops of wax dripped on to her bare skin and mingled with the blood that seemed to be everywhere, staining the bed linen with big, red blotches.

At last she went limp and lifeless on the bed and I was quite out of breath now that it was all over.

I took the tin opener out into the kitchen. Its claw was clogged with congealed blood, but a quick rinse under the hot tap cleaned it up beautifully. I put it back where I had found it and went back into the bedroom. I put the fallen eiderdown neatly over the body, which was terribly red and messy, and then left the house.

I am feeling very pleased with myself but physically exhausted. I hope things will be a little easier tomorrow night.

May 30th

After breakfast this morning, I went out and bought a large knife and a coil of rope. After last night's little difficulty I wanted to be prepared for tonight. Tonight, when I exterminate my third victim.

If only Mother could have seen me! The way that I picked the girl up in the coffee bar and escorted her back to her one-room flat where she lived. I am used to doing this by now, so I didn't find it so repulsive as I did at first.

I even helped her to undress this time. I undid her bra and slipped off her black nylon knickers. I confess that I did feel a little excited by the sight of her at first, but than I remembered what Mother said and everything was all right again.

She had her back to me when I took the rope out of my jacket pocket. As quick as a flash, I threw it over her shoulders, pulled her down on to the bed and secured her tightly. I then took off my belt and beat her as hard as I could. Just as Mother used to beat me when I was bad – to punish me. And she needed punishing for being so sinful and evil.

I carried on until my arm ached and big, moist red weals appeared on her body. She had stopped screaming by this time and was now babbling pleas for mercy. Mercy! Mercy my arse! Why should I show mercy for the likes of her? Little tart! She was bad – real bad – like they all are. Mother said so and she was right.

And now I had to finish the job completely. I took the knife and sank the stainless-steel blade into her flesh. I felt it grate against a bone and blood welled over her skin and on to the bedclothes in thick red clots. Her stomach gaped open and some of its contents spilled out in glistening crimson coils.

I arrived home tired and spent. Murder really does take a lot out of you. But that's the way it is. These things have to be done.

May 31st

There has been a change in my plans. I shall not go out looking for my fourth victim tonight.

A police announcement has just been given on the radio. They are looking for a homicidal killer who has murdered three women. I know it's me that they're after. The stupid fools can't see why I did what I did. They can't see that my job was to rid society of those disgusting trollops.

But I shan't do anything for them any more. Why should I? Why should I when they don't understand? Mother is the only one who would understand and so I must go to her.

I have sharpened the knife in readiness and I hope that my hand will be steady as I draw the blade across my throat. My one wish is that I will not die at once, but remain conscious long enough to offer up one last prayer for Mother, as I die in a crimson glory that will be a token of the good work I have left unfinished.

Ashes to Ashes

Alan Hillery

Doctor Frank Morrow raised his head wearily from his micro-
scope and sighed; the day had been warm and as the hands of
his expensive watch crept round to seven-thirty, the effort of
the day's work weighed heavily on his brain. Joyce Williams,
his assistant, had long since left the building, leaving Morrow
alone in the laboratory, with nothing to break the silence save the
scratching of the caged animals he used in his work.

He was a tall man, gaunt, whose greying hair betrayed his
fifty-five years, his hands small, neat, nimble, a surgeon's hands,
as indeed he had been for fifteen years before forsaking the
scalpel to concentrate on a study of a different nature, the
application of anaesthetics to organ transplants. So successful
was he in this field that it was now possible for him to totally
immobilize, in its living state, any organ of the human body, for
an indefinite period, to be used in future transplant operations,
and all this at a cost to the authorities of half the deep-freezing
technique he had outdated, but now he was tired – God! he was
tired.

Straightening from his bench, he gently removed his spectacles
and cupped his hands over his weary eyes.

It had, he reckoned, been going on for some six months now, six
long months since that first night he had worked late at the
hospital. He had decided to stop taking the car to the laboratory,
partly because of the amount of traffic in the town, and partly
because he felt he needed the exercise. After calling at his club
for his usual hour's relaxation with a whisky and *The Times*

crossword he made his way home to the rambling Georgian house he shared with Melanie, his wife.

Morrow had married late in life, most of his early years being spent in study, the truth being that until he met Melanie, women had not figured in his existence at all, except as faceless beings behind surgical masks at countless operations, or peroxide blondes serving him whisky and sodas from behind leather-clad bars.

Melanie had been different, true she was his junior by twenty-five years, but somehow this age gap seemed immaterial, they were irresistibly drawn together and for the first and only time in his studious life, Dr Frank Morrow was in love – hopelessly, completely, and totally in love. Their marriage had received the blessing of the Church and the happy pair had settled into a life of domesticity in which Morrow found complete happiness. A new dimension opened to him – parties, dinners, social functions of every description through which the rejuvenated doctor glided with consummate ease.

As he had walked up the curving drive to the front door, he had been surprised to see that it was already open, and a young man was standing on the steps speaking to a figure silhouetted in the light from the hall beyond. Melanie's voice floated over the night air.

'Yes, Robert, thank you, it was wonderful. Yes, please come tomorrow night again. He won't be home till nine, so we can have three hours alone.'

The words had cut deep into Morrow's soul and, standing rooted in the rhododendron bushes, he watched numbly as the youth crunched past him along the gravel path, his steps echoing the pounding of the wretched doctor's heart as he disappeared into the darkness.

That had been the first time, and since then there had been others – many others, nights of torture for Morrow, alone in his laboratory, his mind wracked by thoughts of Melanie and the youth – alone in the house – his house – his home. Nights when the doctor had lurked in the garden and watched as the youth and Melanie said their goodbyes; but now he had suffered enough, and slowly a new resolve took possession of him. He dimmed the laboratory lights, retired to his small office and began making notes. One hour later he left the building, a new spring in his step, and a satisfied smile on his face.

It was a week later that Melanie saw it. She and the doctor were having breakfast, and after scanning the fashion and society pages in the morning paper her eyes fell on the Births, Deaths and Marriages column. She read it three times, unbelieving – her eyes were playing tricks surely, yet no! there it was, under the heading Deaths:

MORROW – MELANIE, aged 30, suddenly, at home, beloved wife of Dr Frank Morrow – funeral 11 AM private, 15th, no flowers by request.

'Frank,' she said in a small voice, 'have you seen this?'

'Certainly, darling,' he replied absently, 'it was I who inserted it.'

'But Frank,' panic rising within her, 'what does it mean? Is it some sort of joke?'

'Oh no, Melanie my sweet, it's no joke,' purred the doctor.

'But why? What does . . .' The words were cut off by the sharp snap of breaking teeth as Morrow's fist smashed into her mouth.

He carried his wife's unconscious body into his study and laid it gently on a couch, then with great deliberation he took a hypodermic syringe from his desk, and, after checking his watch, he carefully filled it and injected the contents into a vein directly above the heart.

'There, my faithless little bitch,' he murmured 'that should keep you quiet until the time is right.'

The undertakers arrived a short while later and after a few words of consolation for the bereaved husband, methodically set about their macabre duties. Morrow, waiting in the next room felt a pang of anxiety lest they should find something amiss, but the injection had done its work well, and all the two sombrely-dressed figures saw was a rigid corpse with the usual pallor of death upon it, as indeed, too, did the ancient, drink-sodden medical practitioner who interrupted their work to issue the required death certificate.

Presently, their work completed, the undertakers left, and Morrow, alone again, looked upon his wife, now wrapped in her shroud, her copper hair framing her pale face amid the white drapes of the casket. He smiled to himself and, after gently drawing back the silken sheets, using thick surgical thread, proceeded to stitch her arms across her breasts, and her thighs, feet, and lips together. He was quick, as though completing a successful operation, and after expertly snipping the protruding ends of thread, replaced the sheets, and poured himself a drink.

The funeral itself was quiet, a few friends, mostly the deceased's, who shook their heads, wrung their hands, and dried their eyes, in the best manner of mourners, and at the conclusion of the short service the cortège moved two miles into town to the municipal crematorium. Here the casket was placed on the catafalque, the minister's voice droned the required words, and at the appropriate moment an invisible hand set the retracting machinery in motion and the coffin sank from view. Deep below in the cremating room the seedy little attendant watched the coffin sink towards him.

'Business is brisk', he wheezed to himself. 'If the damned authorities put me on piece work, I'd be a rich man.'

He cackled at his own joke, and, spitting on his hands, wheeled the coffin to the gaping door of the oven, pushed it inside and slammed the steel door shut with a resounding clang which was heard throughout the now-empty building.

Melanie heard it; it was in fact the first thing she did hear as the effects of the injection wore off and her mind swam back to consciousness. At first she did not comprehend, she felt restricted – her arms, mouth, legs, and feet, the darkness, and the confines of the wooden box in which she lay. She tried to open her mouth to cry out, and as the stitches pulled at her lips the revolting truth stabbed through her – the obituary in the morning paper – her husband's fist in her face – the ever-increasing heat. Great God! she was in a coffin and being cremated alive! Blind panic possessed her, she writhed and struggled like a soul in torment, breaking and tearing her skin, ripping great gouts of flesh from her body where the stitches held, bathing herself in warm blood which sizzled in the now-intense heat within the coffin. It was too late, the flames by this time had eaten through the thin wood, and were attacking her body – blistering, reddening, blackening, charring her once milk-white flesh – her last conscious experience was of two thick viscous streams edging their way down her burning face as her eyeballs melted.

One hour later, the attendant laid aside his newspaper and, singing to himself, switched off the gas jets, opened the oven door, and casually raked out the ashes.

The hall clock was chiming five as Dr Frank Morrow poured his fourth double whisky of the afternoon. It had, he told himself been a very successful day – rid once and for all of the unfaithful woman he had married – now he could really get back to work – after all, who could really concentrate on important things with a wife who couldn't be content with one man? He took a sip at the golden liquid, lay back in his chair, closed his eyes, and smiled. A sharp rap on the front door startled him, who could be calling at this hour, not another busybody neighbour offering condolences?

On the steps stood Robert, Melanie's secret visitor, with a long, flat square parcel beneath his arm.

'Good evening, Doctor,' the youth smiled stepping into the hall. 'I think this is what you've been waiting for.'

'Waiting for?' snapped the doctor. 'What on earth do you mean?'

'Why, your surprise birthday gift from your wife.'

He unwrapped the parcel to reveal an exquisite portrait of Melanie, every feature perfect, every dancing highlight in her copper hair shining.

'You see,' the youth explained. 'I'm a freelance artist and your wife commissioned me to paint her portrait for you as a birthday gift – I had to work at night while you were at the laboratory so that you wouldn't find out. It's taken me six months, but it will be worth it if you're satisfied.'

The room spun crazily before Morrow's eyes, he opened his mouth to speak, but as he did so, his eye fell upon the inscription in the bottom corner of the painting, it read:

To Frank, my only love, from Melanie.

The Terrapin

Patricia Highsmith

Victor heard the elevator door open, his mother's quick foot-steps in the hall, and he flipped his book shut. He shoved it under the sofa pillow out of sight, and winced as he heard it slip between sofa and wall and fall to the floor with a thud. Her key was in the lock.

'Hello, Vee-ector-r!' she cried, raising one arm in the air. Her other arm circled a big brown paper-bag, her hand held a cluster of little bags. 'I have been to my publisher and to the market and also to the fish market,' she told him. 'Why aren't you out playing? It's a lovely, lovely day!'

'I was out,' he said. 'For a little while. I got cold.'

'Ugh!' She was unloading the grocery bag in the tiny kitchen off the foyer. 'You are seeck, you know that? In the month of October, you are cold? I see all kinds of children playing on the sidewalk. Even, I think, that boy you like. What's his name?'

'I don't know,' Victor said. His mother wasn't really listening, anyway. He pushed his hands into the pockets of his short, too-small shorts, making them tighter than ever, and walked aimless-ly around the living-room, looking down at his heavy, scuffed shoes. At least his mother had to buy him shoes that fitted him, and he rather liked these shoes, because they had the thickest soles of any he had ever owned, and they had heavy toes that rose up a little, like mountain climbers' shoes. Victor paused at the window and looked straight out at a toast-coloured apartment building across Third Avenue. He and his mother lived on the eighteenth floor, next to the top floor where the penthouses were. The building across the street was even taller than this one. Victor had liked their Riverside Drive apartment better. He had liked the school he had gone to there better. Here

they laughed at his clothes. In the other school, they had finally
got tired of laughing at them.

'You don't want to go out?' asked his mother, coming into the
living-room, wiping her hands briskly on a paper bag. She sniffed
her palms. 'Ugh! That stee-enk!'

'No, Mama,' Victor said patiently.

'Today is Saturday.'

'I know.'

'Can you say the days of the week?'

'Of course.'

'Say them.'

'I don't want to say them. I know them.' His eyes began to
sting around the edges with tears. 'I've known them for years.
Years and years. Kids five years old can say the days of the
week.'

But his mother was not listening. She was bending over the
drawing-table in the corner of the room. She had worked late on
something last night. On his sofa bed in the opposite corner of
the room, Victor had not been able to sleep until two in the
morning, when his mother had gone to bed on the studio
couch.

'Come here, Veector. Did you see this?'

Victor came on dragging feet, hands still in his pockets. No,
he hadn't even glanced at her drawing-board this morning,
hadn't wanted to.

'This is Pedro, the little donkey. I invented him last night.
What do you think? And this is Miguel, the little Mexican boy
who rides him. They ride and ride all over Mexico, and Miguel
thinks they are lost, but Pedro knows the way home all the time,
and . . .'

Victor did not listen. He deliberately shut his ears in a way he
had learned to do from many years of practice, but boredom,
frustration – he knew the word frustration, had read all about it –
clamped his shoulders, weighed like a stone in his body, pressed
hatred and tears up to his eyes, as if a volcano were churning in
him. He had hoped his mother might take a hint from his saying
that he was cold in his silly short shorts. He had hoped his
mother might remember what he had told her, that the fellow

he had wanted to get acquainted with downstairs, a fellow who looked about his own age, eleven, had laughed at his short pants on Monday afternoon. *They make you wear your kid brother's pants or something?* Victor had drifted away, mortified. What if the fellow knew he didn't even own any longer pants, not even a pair of knickers, much less *long* pants, even blue jeans! His mother, for some cock-eyed reason, wanted him to look 'French', and made him wear short shorts and stockings that came to just below his knees, and dopey shirts with round collars. His mother wanted him to stay about six years old, for ever, all his life. She liked to test out her drawings on him. *Veector is my sounding board*, she sometimes said to her friends. *I show my drawings to Veector and I know if children will like them.* Often Victor said he liked stories that he did not like, or drawings that he was indifferent to, because he felt sorry for his mother and because it put her in a better mood if he said he liked them. He was quite tired now of children's book illustrations, if he had ever in his life liked them – he really couldn't remember – and now he had two favourites: Howard Pyle's illustrations in some of Robert Louis Stevenson's books and Cruikshank's in Dickens. It was too bad, Victor thought, that he was absolutely the last person of whom his mother should have asked an opinion, because he simply *hated* children's illustrations. And it was a wonder his mother didn't see this, because she hadn't sold any illustrations for books for years and years, not since *Wimple-Dimple*, a book whose jacket was all torn and turning yellow now from age, which sat in the centre of the bookshelf in a little cleared spot, propped up against the back of the bookcase so everyone could see it. Victor had been seven years old when that book was printed. His mother liked to tell people and remind him, too, that he had told her what he wanted to see her draw, had watched her make every drawing, had shown his opinion by laughing or not, and that she had been absolutely guided by him. Victor doubted this very much, because first of all the story was somebody else's and had been written before his mother did the drawings, and her drawings had had to follow the story, naturally. Since then, his mother had done only a few illustrations now and then for magazines for children, how to make paper pumpkins and black paper cats for Hallowe'en and things like that, though she took her portfolio around to publishers all the time. Their income came from his father, who was a wealthy businessman in France, an exporter of perfumes. His mother said he was very wealthy and very handsome. But he had married again, he never wrote, and Victor had no interest in him, didn't even care if he never saw a picture of him, and he never had. His father was French with some Polish, and his mother was Hungarian with some French. The word Hungarian made Victor think of gypsies, but when he had asked his mother once, she had said emphatically that she hadn't any gypsy blood, and she had been annoyed that Victor brought the question up.

And now she was sounding him out again, poking him in the ribs to make him wake up, as she repeated:

'Listen to me! Which do you like better, Veector? "In all Mexico there was no bur-r-ro as wise as Miguel's Pedro", or "Miguel's Pedro was the wisest bur-r-ro in all Mexico"?'

'I think – I like it the first way better.'

'Which way is that?' demanded his mother, thumping her palm down on the illustration.

Victor tried to remember the wording, but realized he was only staring at the pencil smudges, the thumbprints on the edges of his mother's illustration board. The coloured drawing in the centre did not interest him at all. He was not-thinking. This was a frequent, familiar sensation to him now, there was something exciting and important about not-thinking, Victor felt, and he thought one day he would find something about it – perhaps under another name – in the public library or in the psychology books around the house that he browsed in when his mother was out.

'Veec-tor! What are you doing?'

'Nothing, Mama!'

'That is exactly it! Nothing! Can you not even *think*?'

A warm shame spread through him. It was as if his mother read his thoughts about not-thinking. 'I am thinking,' he protested. 'I'm thinking about *not*-thinking.' His tone was defiant. What could she do about it, after all?

'About what?' Her black, curly head tilted, her mascaraed eyes narrowed at him.

'Not-thinking.'

His mother put her jewelled hands on her hips. 'Do you know, Veec-tor, you are a little bit strange in the head?' She nodded. 'You are seeck. Psychologically seeck. And retarded, do you know that? You have the behaviour of a leetle boy five years old,' she said slowly and weightily. 'It is just as well you spend your Saturdays indoors. Who knows if you would not walk in front of a car, eh? But that is why I love you, little Veec-tor.' She put her arm around his shoulders, pulled him against her and for an instant Victor's nose pressed into her large, soft bosom. She was wearing her flesh-coloured dress, the one you could see through a little where her breast stretched it out.

Victor jerked his head away in a confusion of emotions. He did not know if he wanted to laugh or cry.

His mother was laughing gaily, her head back. 'Seeck you are! Look at you! My lee-tle boy still, lee-tle short pants – Ha! Ha!'

Now the tears showed in his eyes, he supposed, and his mother acted as if she were enjoying it! Victor turned his head away so she would not see his eyes. Then suddenly he faced her. 'Do you think I like these pants? *You* like them, not me, so why do you have to make fun of them?'

'A lee-tle boy who's crying!' she went on, laughing.

Victor made a dash for the bathroom, then swerved away and dived onto the sofa, his face towards the pillows. He shut his eyes tight and opened his mouth, crying but not-crying in a way he had learned through practice also. With his mouth open, his throat tight, not breathing for nearly a minute, he could some-how get the satisfaction of crying, screaming even, without any-body knowing it. He pushed his nose, his open mouth, his teeth, against the tomato-red sofa pillow, and though his mother's voice went on in a lazily mocking tone, and her laughter went on, he imagined that it was getting fainter and more distant from him. He imagined, rigid in every muscle, that he was suffering the absolute worst that any human being could suffer.

He imagined that he was dying. But he did not think of death as an escape, only as a concentrated and painful incident. This was the climax of his not-crying. Then he breathed again, and his mother's voice intruded:

'Did you hear me? – *Did you hear me?* Mrs Badzerkian is coming for tea. I want you to wash your face and put on a clean shirt. I want you to recite something for her. Now what are you going to recite?'

'"In winter when I go to bed,"' said Victor. She was making him memorize every poem in *A Child's Garden of Verses*. He had said the first one that came into his head, and now there was an argument, because he had recited that one the last time. 'I said it, because I couldn't think of any other one right off the bat!' Victor shouted.

'Don't yell at me!' his mother cried, storming across the room at him.

She slapped his face before he knew what was happening.

He was up on one elbow on the sofa, on his back, his long, knobbly-kneed legs splayed out in front of him. All right, he thought, if that's the way it is, that's the way it is. He looked at her with loathing. He would not show the slap had hurt, that it still stung. No more tears for today, he swore, no more even not-crying. He would finish the day, go through the tea, like a stone, like a soldier, not wincing. His mother paced around the room, turning one of her rings round and round, glancing at him from time to time, looking quickly away from him. But his eyes were steady on her. He was not afraid. She could even slap him again and he wouldn't care.

At last, she announced that she was going to wash her hair, and she went into the bathroom.

Victor got up from the sofa and wandered across the room. He wished he had a room of his own to go to. In the apartment on Riverside Drive, there had been three rooms, a living-room, and his and his mother's rooms. When she was in the living-room, he had been able to go into his bedroom and vice versa, but here . . . They were going to tear down the old building they had lived in on Riverside Drive. It was not a pleasant thing for Victor to think about. Suddenly remembering the book that had fallen, he pulled out the sofa and reached for it. It was Menninger's *The Human Mind*, full of fascinating case histories of people. Victor put it back on the bookshelf between an astrology book and *How to Draw*. His mother did not like him to read psychology books, but Victor loved them, especially ones with case histories in them. The people in the case histories did what they wanted to do. They were natural. Nobody bossed them. At the local branch library, he spent hours browsing through the psychology shelves. They were in the adults' section, but the librarian did not mind his sitting at the tables there, because he was quiet.

Victor went into the kitchen and got a glass of water. As he was standing there drinking it, he heard a scratching noise coming from one of the paper bags on the counter. A mouse, he thought, but when he moved a couple of the bags, he didn't see any mouse. The scratching was coming from inside one of the bags. Gingerly, he opened the bag with his fingers, and waited for something to jump out. Looking in, he saw a white paper carton. He pulled it out slowly. Its bottom was damp. It opened like a pastry box. Victor jumped in surprise. It was a turtle on its back, a live turtle. It was wriggling its legs in the air, trying to turn over. Victor moistened his lips, and frowning with concentration, took the turtle by its sides with both hands, turned him over and let him down gently into the box again. The turtle drew in its feet then, and its head stretched up a little and it looked straight at him. Victor smiled. Why hadn't his mother told him she'd brought him a present? A live turtle. Victor's eyes glazed with anticipation as he thought of taking the turtle down, maybe with a leash around its neck, to show the fellow who'd laughed at his short pants. He might change his mind about being friends with him, if he found he owned a turtle.

'Hey, Mama! Mama!' Victor yelled at the bathroom door. 'You brought me a tur-rtle?'

'A what?' The water shut off.

'A turtle! In the kitchen!' Victor had been jumping up and down in the hall. He stopped.

His mother had hesitated, too. The water came on again,

and she said in a shrill tone, '*C'est une terrapène! Pour un ragoût!*'

Victor understood, and a small chill went over him because his mother had spoken in French. His mother addressed him in French when she was giving an order that had to be obeyed, or when she anticipated resistance from him. So the terrapin was for a stew. Victor nodded to himself with a stunned resignation, and went back to the kitchen. For a stew. Well, the terrapin was not long for this world, as they say. What did a terrapin like to eat? Lettuce? Raw bacon? Boiled potato? Victor peered into the refrigerator.

He held a piece of lettuce near the terrapin's horny mouth. The terrapin did not open its mouth, but it looked at him. Victor held the lettuce near the two little dots of its nostrils, but if the terrapin smelled it, it showed no interest. Victor looked under the sink and pulled out a large wash pan. He put two inches of water into it. Then he gently dumped the terrapin into the pan. The terrapin paddled for a few seconds, as if it had to swim, then finding that its stomach sat on the bottom of the pan, it stopped, and drew its feet in. Victor got down on his knees and studied the terrapin's face. Its upper lip overhung the lower, giving it a rather stubborn and unfriendly expression, but its eyes – they were bright and shining. Victor smiled when he looked hard at them.

'Okay, *monsieur terrapène*,' he said, 'just tell me what you'd like to eat and we'll get it for you! – Maybe some tuna?'

They had had tuna-fish salad yesterday for dinner, and there was a small bowl of it left over. Victor got a little chunk of it in his fingers and presented it to the terrapin. The terrapin was not interested. Victor looked around the kitchen, wondering, then seeing the sunlight on the floor of the living-room, he picked up the pan and carried it to the living-room and set it down so the sunlight would fall on the terrapin's back. All turtles liked sunlight, Victor thought. He lay down on the floor on his side, propped up on an elbow. The terrapin stared at him for a moment, then very slowly and with an air of forethought and caution, put out its legs and advanced, found the circular boundary of the pan, and moved to the right, half its body out of the shallow water. It wanted to get out, and Victor took it in one hand, by the sides, and said:

'You can come out and have a little walk.'

He smiled as the terrapin started to disappear under the sofa. He caught it easily, because it moved so slowly. When he put it down on the carpet, it was quite still, as if it had withdrawn a little to think what it should do next, where it should go. It was a brownish green. Looking at it, Victor thought of river bottoms, of river water flowing. Or maybe oceans. Where did terrapins come from? He jumped up and went to the dictionary on the bookshelf. The dictionary had a picture of a terrapin, but it was a dull, black and white drawing, not so pretty as the live one. He learned nothing except that the name was of Algonquian origin, that the terrapin lived in fresh or brackish water, and that it was edible. Edible. Well, that was bad luck. Victor thought. But he was not going to eat any *terrapène* tonight. It would be all for his mother, that *ragoût*, and even if she slapped him and made him learn an extra two or three poems, he would not eat any terrapin tonight.

His mother came out of the bathroom. 'What are you doing there? – Veec-tor?'

Victor put the dictionary back on the shelf. His mother had seen the pan. 'I'm looking at the terrapin,' he said, then realized the terrapin had disappeared. He got down on hands and knees and looked under the sofa.

'Don't put him on the furniture. He makes spots,' said his mother. She was standing in the foyer, rubbing her hair vigorously with a towel.

Victor found the terrapin between the wastebasket and the wall. He put him back in the pan.

'Have you changed your shirt?' asked his mother.

Victor changed his shirt, and then at his mother's order sat down on the sofa with *A Child's Garden of Verses* and tackled another poem, a brand-new one for Mrs Badzerkian. He learned two lines at a time, reading it aloud in a soft voice to himself, then repeating it, then putting two, four and six lines together, until he had the whole thing. He recited it to the terrapin. Then Victor asked his mother if he could play with the terrapin in the bathtub.

'No! And get your shirt all splashed?'

'I can put on my other shirt.'

'No! It's nearly four o'clock now. Get that pan out of the living-room!'

Victor carried the pan back to the kitchen. His mother took the terrapin quite fearlessly out of the pan, put it back into the white paper box, closed its lid, and stuck the box in the refrigerator. Victor jumped a little as the refrigerator door slammed. It would be awfully cold in there for the terrapin. But then, he supposed, fresh or brackish water was cold now and then, too.

'Veector, cut the lemon,' said his mother. She was preparing the big round tray with cups and saucers. The water was boiling in the kettle.

Mrs Badzerkian was prompt as usual, and his mother poured the tea as soon as she had deposited her coat and pocketbook on the foyer chair and sat down. Mrs Badzerkian smelled of cloves. She had a small, straight mouth and a thin moustache on her upper lip which fascinated Victor, as he had never seen one on a woman before, not one at such short range, anyway. He never had mentioned Mrs Badzerkian's moustache to his mother, knowing it was considered ugly, but in a strange way, her moustache was the thing he liked best about her. The rest of her was dull, uninteresting, and vaguely unfriendly. She always pretended to listen carefully to his poetry recitals, but he felt that she fidgeted, thought of other things while he spoke, and was glad when it was over. Today, Victor recited very well and without any hesitation, standing in the middle of the living-room floor and facing the two women, who were then having their second cups of tea.

'Très bien,' said his mother. 'Now you may have a cookie.'

Victor chose from the plate a small round cookie with a drop of orange goo in its centre. He kept his knees close together when he sat down. He always felt Mrs Badzerkian looked at his knees and with distaste. He often wished she would make some remark to his mother about his being old enough for long pants, but she never had, at least not within his hearing. Victor learned from his mother's conversation with Mrs Badzerkian that the Lorentzes were coming for dinner tomorrow evening. It was probably for them that the terrapin stew was going to be made. Victor was glad that he would have the terrapin one more day to play with. Tomorrow morning, he thought, he would ask his mother if he could take the terrapin down on the sidewalk for a while, either on a leash or in the paper box, if his mother insisted.

'— like a chi-ild!' his mother was saying, laughing, with a glance at him, and Mrs Badzerkian smiled shrewdly at him with her small, tight mouth.

Victor had been excused, and was sitting across the room with a book on the studio couch. His mother was telling Mrs Badzerkian how he had played with the terrapin. Victor frowned down at his book, pretending not to hear. His mother did not like him to open his mouth to her or her guests once he had been excused. But now she was calling him her 'lee-tle ba-aby Veec-tor . . .'

He stood up with his finger in the place in his book. 'I don't see why it's childish to look at a terrapin!' he said, flushing with sudden anger. 'They are very interesting animals, they —'

His mother interrupted him with a laugh, but at once the laugh disappeared and she said sternly, 'Veector, I thought I had excused you. Isn't that correct?'

He hesitated, seeing in a flash the scene that was going to take place when Mrs Badzerkian had left. 'Yes, Mama. I'm sorry,' he said. Then he sat down and bent over his book again.

Twenty minutes later, Mrs Badzerkian left. His mother scolded him for being rude, but it was not a five- or ten-minute scolding of the kind he had expected. It lasted hardly two minutes. She had forgotten to buy cream, and she wanted Victor to go downstairs and get some. Victor put on his grey woollen jacket and went out. He always felt embarrassed and conspicuous in the jacket, because it came just a little bit below his short pants, and he looked as if he had nothing on underneath the coat.

Victor looked around for Frank on the sidewalk, but he didn't see him. He crossed Third Avenue and went to a delicatessen in the big building that he could see from the living-room window.

On his way back, he saw Frank walking along the sidewalk, bouncing a ball. Now Victor went right up to him.

'Hey,' Victor said. 'I've got a terrapin upstairs.'

'A what?' Frank caught the ball and stopped.

'A terrapin. You know, like a turtle. I'll bring him down tomorrow morning and show you, if you're around. He's pretty big.'

'Yeah?—Why don't you bring him down now?'

'Because we're gonna eat now,' said Victor. 'See you.' He went into his building. He felt he had achieved something. Frank had looked really interested. Victor wished he could bring the terrapin down now, but his mother never liked him to go out after dark, and it was practically dark now.

When Victor got upstairs, his mother was still in the kitchen. Eggs were boiling and she had put a big pot of water on a back burner. 'You took him out again!' Victor said, seeing the terrapin's box on the counter.

'Yes, I prepare the stew tonight,' said his mother. 'That is why I need the cream.'

Victor looked at her. 'You're going to— You have to kill it tonight?'

'Yes, my little one. Tonight.' She jiggled the pot of eggs.

'Mama, can I take him downstairs to show Frank?' Victor asked quickly. 'Just for five minutes, Mama. Frank's down there now.'

'Who is Frank?'

'He's that fellow you asked me about today. The blond fellow we always see. Please, Mama.'

His mother's black eyebrows frowned. 'Take the *terrapène* downstairs? Certainly not. Don't be absurd, my baby! The *terrapène* is not a toy!'

Victor tried to think of some other lever of persuasion. He had not removed his coat. 'You wanted me to get acquainted with Frank —'

'Yes. What has that got to do with a terrapin?'

The water on the back burner began to boil.

'You see, I promised him I'd —' Victor watched his mother lift the terrapin from the box, and as she dropped it into the boiling water, his mouth fell open. '*Mama!*'

'What is this? What is this noise?'

Victor, open-mouthed, stared at the terrapin whose legs were now racing against the steep sides of the pot. The terrapin's mouth opened, its eyes looked directly at Victor for an instant, its head arched back in torture, the open mouth sank beneath the seething water – and that was the end. Victor blinked. It was dead. He came closer, saw the four legs and the tail stretched out in the water, its head. He looked at his mother.

She was drying her hands on a towel. She glanced at him, then said, 'Ugh!' She smelled her hands, then hung the towel back.

'Did you have to kill him like that?'

'How else? The same way you kill a lobster. Don't you know that? It doesn't hurt them.'

He stared at her. When she started to touch him, he stepped back. He thought of the terrapin's wide open mouth, and his eyes suddenly flooded with tears. Maybe the terrapin had been screaming and it hadn't been heard over the bubbling of the water. The terrapin had looked at him, wanting him to pull him out, and he hadn't moved to help him. His mother had tricked him, done it so fast, he couldn't save him. He stepped back again. 'No, don't touch me!'

His mother slapped his face, hard and quickly.

Victor set his jaw. Then he about-faced and went to the closet and threw his jacket onto a hanger and hung it up. He went into the living-room and fell down on the sofa. He was not crying now, but his mouth opened against the sofa pillow. Then he remembered the terrapin's mouth and he closed his lips. The terrapin had suffered, otherwise it would not have moved its legs so terribly fast to get out. Then he wept, soundlessly as the terrapin, his mouth open. He put both hands over his face, so as not to wet the sofa. After a long while, he got up. In the kitchen, his mother was humming, and every few minutes he heard her quick, firm steps as she went about her work. Victor had set his teeth again. He walked slowly to the kitchen doorway.

The terrapin was out on the wooden chopping board, and his mother, after a glance at him, still humming, took a knife and bore down on its blade, cutting off the terrapin's little nails.

Victor half closed his eyes, but he watched steadily. The nails, with bits of skin attached to them, his mother scooped off the board into her palm and dumped into the garbage bag. Then she turned the terrapin onto its back and with the same sharp, pointed knife, she began to cut away the pale bottom shell. The terrapin's neck was bent sideways. Victor wanted to look away, but still he stared. Now the terrapin's insides were all exposed, red and white and greenish. Victor did not listen to what his mother was saying, about cooking terrapins in Europe, before he was born. Her voice was gentle and soothing, not at all like what she was doing.

'All right, don't look at me like that!' she suddenly threw at him, stomping her foot. 'What's the matter with you? Are you crazy? Yes, I think so! You are seeck, you know that?'

Victor could not touch any of his supper, and his mother could not force him to, even though she shook him by the shoulders and threatened to slap him. They had creamed chipped beef on toast. Victor did not say a word. He felt very remote from his mother, even when she screamed right into his face. He felt very odd, the way he did sometimes when he was sick at his stomach, but he was not sick at his stomach. When they went to bed, he felt afraid of the dark. He saw the terrapin's face very large, its mouth open, its eyes wide and full of pain. Victor wished he could walk out the window and float, go anywhere he wanted to, disappear, yet be everywhere. He imagined his mother's hands on his shoulders, jerking him back, if he tried to step out the window. He hated his mother.

He got up and went quietly into the kitchen. The kitchen was absolutely dark, as there was no window, but he put his hand accurately on the knife rack and felt gently for the knife he wanted. He thought of the terrapin, in little pieces now, all mixed up in the sauce of cream and egg yolks and sherry in the pot in the refrigerator.

His mother's cry was not silent; it seemed to tear his ears off. His second blow was in her body, and then he stabbed her throat again. Only tiredness made him stop, and by then people were trying to bump the door in. Victor at last walked to the door, pulled the chain bolt back, and opened it for them.

He was taken to a large, old building full of nurses and doctors. Victor was very quiet and did everything he was asked to do, and answered the questions they put to him, but only those questions, and since they didn't ask him anything about a terrapin, he did not bring it up.

Sergeant Lacey Demonstrates

Norman P. Kaufman

'Both my arms and legs are broken: what would you do about it – Billett?'

Private Billett was red of hair, gangling of body, slow of speech and slower of action. 'We-e-ell, sir, I – that is, I imagine we'd have to —'

Lacey waved him to silence. 'There is no room for imagination in this man's army, Billett – we have a set procedure to adopt, a list of strictly-laid-down rules to observe.' He gestured at the pebbled, lonely beach, at the rocks lofting high above their heads.

'We're not playing games, laddie,' he went on, while Billett shifted in discomfort. 'We've all left kindergarten, remember? Now –' his tone sharpened '– listen to me and listen good, all of you. Because this isn't make-believe, you know; accidents like this could really happen, and I'm here to show you how to go about things the right way.' The wind blew the words back in his face; the sea boiled up into white-plumed waves. 'Shall we get on with it then?' he finished, mock-polite.

They waited, twelve or fourteen unwilling Privates, watching, hating . . . 'Here you, Johnston, you carry on, eh?' Lacey lifted interrogatory eyebrows. 'What would you do if you found me as I described?'

'Well sir —' Johnston hesitated; then, seeing his superior's jaw tighten, he blundered on: 'We'd make sure you weren't moved until the proper equipment had been brought to you – a stretcher and blankets and the necessary strapping. Oh, and morphine —'

'Oh, and morphine!' Lacey's sneer was like a blow in the face, and Johnston stepped back a pace. 'Oh, and morphine!' the Sergeant repeated. 'Here am I with broken limbs, and you treat the morphine as an afterthought! Don't you reckon it hurts, then? Would you like me to break your leg, maybe, to convince you?' His laughter was humorless, a squeal of derisive scorn.

And then suddenly his lips were twisted in exasperation. 'I've had my fill of all this yammer-yammer; better to demonstrate the whole thing, then perhaps something will get through the glue round your brains . . .' Johnston stood back; he was a man of middle height, around thirty-six years old and tending to flabbiness. He gestured helplessly, and the young Sergeant laughed his hateful laugh.

'Don't fret, Johnston,' he scoffed. 'I shan't ask you to show the others, I know instinctively you'll botch it— Dover!' he rasped out in unexpected staccato, and the man named leaped in pure fright.

'Me, sir?' His voice was a shocked whisper, his eyes dilated in anticipatory fear; and Lacey nodded blandly.

'You sir,' he affirmed. 'Let's see how you shape up – let's start pretending, shall we?' He lowered himself full-stretch on to the pebbled beach. 'Now then, Dover,' he went on, 'I've been climbing the north face of the tor, which you see above us. I have slipped and fallen on to this beach, and all my limbs are broken . . . Well, Dover?'

Private Walter Dover, eighteen years old, personification of meekness, approached nervously, wishing whole-heartedly that the world would come to an end, however temporarily. 'Could you – ah – would you move your feet together, sir – Sergeant – please? . . .'

Lacey blew out his cheeks in exaggerated annoyance. 'Move my feet? I can't move at all, man, don't you understand that? Or is it that you just *won't* understand?' His voice was steeped in caustic acid. 'Oh hell, skip it, will you? Go back to sleep, will you? . . . Now then, you, Hillary, let's see what you can do to make things worse, shall we?'

Hillary stepped forward, thin, balding, his pale face expressionless. 'I'll try my best, Sergeant.' He stooped and, with infinite gentleness, he moved Lacey's feet together; and again

with a careful, almost velvet touch, he placed the Sergeant's
arms by his side.

'You've probably broken my limbs twice over, the way you've
handled me,' was the sniffed and perhaps anticipated comment.
But Private Hillary merely smiled a deprecating smile.

'Sorry, sir, I'm only doing my best —'

'Oh don't keep saying that, fellow – get on, get *on*!' Nodding
obediently, the wind gusting the few strands of hair across his
washed-blue eyes, Hillary rolled the Sergeant's lolling body on
to the huge tarpaulin. Lacey grunted emphatically. 'I hope we
can assume,' he suggested sardonically, 'that morphine has been
administered as prescribed?'

'Oh yes, sir.' The Private's tone was ultra-calm, ultra-respect-
ful. 'You may indeed take it that this has been done, Sergeant.'

Lacey grimaced, nettled at the other's unruffled manner. 'Say
so then, in future – and now get on with it, if it's not too much
trouble . . .'

Hillary wrapped the canvas sheet around his Sergeant's
supine form, then eased the stretcher underneath; with Lacey's
jeering gaze on him, the pale, thin Private never faltered, never
flinched. With considerable expertise he strapped the strong
belting firmly around Lacey's mummified figure, thus binding
soldier and stretcher into a single unit. Pausing only to tug
experimentally at the straps, Hillary rose to his feet, his face still
devoid of emotion.

'Finished?' The Sergeant, it appeared, was not impressed. 'I
feel as if a herd of tuskers has trampled me. Do you realize,
Hillary, what the situation demands? Do you realize that I'm
supposed to be a virtual cripple? Do you comprehend what
agony is involved in a case of this type? After all you've been
taught, how many more times? . . .' He broke off, sighing deeply,
searingly.

'Oh what's the use – I'm obviously wasting my time and
breath on a pack of crass idiots – but don't think the matter will
end here: you'll all be going on report for your unconscionable
lack of knowledge.' He jerked his head at the surrounding group.
'There's another beach about half a mile on, past the tor; all
but Hillary get along there now, and wait for me there. That is,

if you don't get lost on the way.' He shook his head. 'The sooner this damn training course is over with, the better I'll like it – now you, Hillary, get me out of this.'

Dover, Johnston, Billett and the rest, visibly depressed by the tongue-lashing sarcasm of their Sergeant, crunched across the pebbles and rocks until they rounded the headland and were lost to sight.

'Come on then, man! What the hell are you fooling around for? I didn't ask you to stare at me, just to untie me! Now quit this mooning about and do as you're told!'

Hillary, polite as ever, smiled again, and knelt by Lacey's helpless body. 'Yes, sir. Sorry, sir. But first I'd like your advice – not your verbal advice, much as I respect it; for as you are aware, sir . . .' Lacey strained to catch the words as the wind reached another soughing peak. '. . . As you know, sir, we're all very forgetful —'

'Damned right you are – I've never known such —'

'Quite, sir. So you'll understand why I want a physical demonstration; I'm sure it would prove of more value . . .' He paused, and Lacey cut in.

'Hillary, will you *immediately* untie these —'

'Now suppose, Sergeant,' Hillary continued, unheeding, 'just for instance, that I'm about to unstrap you and I trip and fall, and I knock myself out – which, by the way, is the reason for this nasty gash in my head . . .' He reached down and scooped up a sharp stone; gritting his teeth, he drew it firmly and carefully along his forehead.

'What the hell —'

'Now then, sir,' the Private interposed gently. 'The other lads have vanished round the headland there, innocently on their way to the adjoining beach, as per your orders. Come to think of it, I'm willing to bet that they're glad to have a respite from your bawling and shouting and your unnecessary nagging and your damned superiority – sir.'

Lacey swallowed hard. 'Hillary —'

'And me – well, as for me, I'm unconscious, am I not? I certainly can't help you, Sergeant. And you're all strapped up, you're completely immobile, aren't you, and you can't expect anybody to hear you in this wind, am I right?' Hillary stared out to sea, his eyes still blank. A thin line of perspiration had formed on his upper lip.

'And now – now the tide is almost completely in; it turns out later that I came to just in time to save myself, after struggling vainly to rescue the helpless Sergeant Lacey . . .'

He got to his feet, the wind rocking his frail body, his thin face veiled in blood. 'We're not playing games, sir,' he stressed firmly. 'This isn't make-believe; accidents like this can really happen —'

He turned and walked slowly up the beach, squatted down about a hundred feet away, his back against the foot of the tor. For some minutes he listened to Lacey's screams; but soon there was nothing but the thunder of the surf.

Borderline

James Jauncey

Harry had an inferiority complex. Well, you see, the trouble was that Harry had been born with a malformed arm. Added to this he was physically small – he had a frail body set off by a disproportionately large head, so that when he walked, his deformed arm dangling uselessly at his side, he looked as if he was about to fall forward, toppled over by his head; so Harry had a stoop.

What made things worse was that all his mates teased him incessantly about it. 'Harry the stump,' they called him. Harry, quite understandably did not appreciate the joke.

'Owzat?' they used to yell when Harry arrived for work in the morning.

'Stumped,' someone would reply, and the yard would echo with coarse laughter . . .

But Harry was grim. 'Trouble is,' he thought, 'I'm inadequate. If I was bigger I could clobber the bastards, but I'm not.' So Harry could only brood.

Harry worked in the sewers. 'Well, I mean,' he had said to himself, 'I look so horrible that the best thing for me is to get a job where at least no one can see me.'

At 8.30 every morning he reported to the yard, and at 8.45 he set off, armed with a five-foot pole for a day's work in the sewers. Harry's job was to take a beat of the sewers each day and check the grills, placed at intervals along the main course, for anything that might have got caught in them; these grills spanned the sewer and consisted of a mesh of iron rods, intended to catch any conglomeration of sewage which might ultimately cause a blockage. When Harry found anything of this nature, he had to try to loosen it with his pole until it broke up sufficiently to flow through the grill.

At 5.30 Harry used to return to the yard, go to the washroom, shove his boiler suit down the laundry chute, shower and dress, ready to catch the six o'clock bus home. Through the steam in the washroom Harry often noticed his mates – they were no more his mates than the man in the moon, but Harry told himself they were – huddled round in groups, and he could not help hear them discussing the petty theft in which they all indulged from time to time. Occasionally one would turn round to cast a pitying glance at Harry, as he laboriously scrubbed himself under the shower, trying hard to look as if he couldn't be less interested. But he was – Harry was interested all right.

One evening Harry was standing in the washroom after a really shocking day: he had nearly fallen in the main sewer in the morning, and had lost his pole in the process; he had lost his temper after excessive ribbing from the others in the lunch break, and had for ten minutes seriously contemplated taking a Charles Atlas course; in the afternoon he had banged his head on a low piece of vaulting. Harry was in no mood for trifling.

As he emerged from the shower and started to dry himself, he noticed the usual discussion was in full swing and through the hissing of the shower he vaguely heard the words: 'night ... knocked off ... fifty nicker ...' Harry moved a little closer. Suddenly one of them swung round on him, and said leeringly:

'Thrilling ain't it 'Arry? Like wot you read in them Sunday papers.' Then turning to the others he sneered, 'Why, I bet 'Arry's never knocked off so much as a bloody acid drop.'

Something went inside Harry's head – he had never felt so humiliated.

'Acid drop,' he thought, 'Christ, I'll show the sods!'

He turned on his heel, dressed, and stalked out.

As Harry stumbled along in the darkness of the sewer, he was, for the first time in his life, really jubilant. He, Harry, had actually done it. Harry the Stump (he could almost laugh about that now) had committed a successful crime – indeed a crime in whose presence the petty theft of his mates would pale into miserable insignificance.

'No more sewers for me,' he thought. 'And as for those crummy, gutless, tuppenny-halfpenny thieves back at the yard – they can take a running jump.'

Harry sighed ecstatically as he groped along the sewer edge, clutching a small sack in his good hand.

'South America, umm . . . yeah, South America, that's where I'll go.' The prospect of South America had always fascinated Harry, ever since he had in his early childhood discovered in an attic, and avidly devoured, a book on the sexual habits of the tribes of the Amazon. 'I'll build meself a socking great palace, get twenty or thirty native tarts and go into retirement where no one will ever bother me again. After all, what's an appearance when you've got the lolly.'

Harry's reverie was rudely disturbed as something large and furry scuttled out of the wall and shot between his legs. Harry nearly lost his balance; as he flailed his arms to prevent himself crashing into the sewer, he momentarily slackened his grip on the sack, and with utter dismay he felt the coarse material whisk through his fingers. There was a split second's silence and then a 'thwlp' as the water closed over the sack.

Harry took all of thirty seconds to regain his composure, and even then the tunnel rang with his oaths. After a further thirty seconds' brain-racking, Harry turned round and retraced his steps to the last grill he had passed, still muttering, 'F—ing rat' as he went.

There, he guessed, rightly as it turned out, the sack would have been swept along the floor of the sewer and would now be caught against the grill. However, the water was too deep for Harry to retrieve it from the edge and, anyway, the sack had fallen well out in the middle of the sewer; so grasping the nearest upright of the grill, he stretched out a foot and placed his toe in a square of the mesh of the grill. Then, pulling himself up with his other hand and placing his other foot likewise in the grill, he edged his way slowly out to the centre of the sewer.

Harry eased himself down till the water was up to his chest, and then taking a deep breath, he submerged and, hanging on with his good hand, stretched down with the other. Twenty seconds later he surfaced gasping for breath and empty-handed; having regained his wind he submerged again. Reaching down, his fingers suddenly brushed a bulky object and as he stretched the extra six inches to grasp the object, the effort caused his left foot to slip off the slimy grill. Trying to save himself, he thrust his good hand through the grill and it was not until he surfaced again, this time clutching the sack, that he realized that his hand was quite immovably wedged in the mesh – no matter how much he tugged and squirmed, it would not come loose.

This time, a shiver of fear shook Harry's body, from the top of his goose-pimpled cranium to the bottom of his size-six waders. He reached out and lobbed the sack onto the footpath, and then eased himself into a more comfortable position to think. The more Harry thought, the more he wished he hadn't; it was quite clear to him that he could by no stretch of the imagination pull himself free and, looking at his watch, he saw that it read 3 AM – no one would be coming down this tunnel until 9 AM, the day after next. Harry's feet were already numb with cold and from time to time he gave an involuntary cough. He managed to kick off his waders and wiggle his toes, but even so, within ten minutes he could not feel them at all.

'Christ,' he thought, 'I'll be a ruddy stiff by breakfast-time at this rate. Harry, me boy, you really have cocked it up this time.'

Suddenly Harry remembered something which made him freeze with terror; he glanced at his watch again and could not suppress a cry. So far he had not really accepted the reality of the situation and had jollied himself along, pretending that it was a dream, and that soon he would wake up in his bed-sit and would see the daylight and hear the traffic.

But this brought it home – bang! Harry's heart missed several beats and then doubled its pace, his skin ran cold and his stomach dropped to his knees. Harry had remembered that every morning at 5 AM they opened the main sluice gates at the centre of the sewers, thus loosing a large volume of water through every tunnel, filling it to the roof and cleaning it thoroughly for the influx of sewage the next morning.

'Oh my Gawd,' Harry gibbered, his arms shaking. 'Oh Gawd,

I've just gotta get out,' he repeated to himself. Fear had chilled his brain and he could not think – only the words 'Gotta get out' ran circles in his head.

While he mumbled to himself, Harry heard a rustling on the footpath, and straining his eyes he made out the shapes of several large furry objects sniffing the sack, their long hairless tails swishing on the ground as they worked.

'You bastards,' he yelled, 'it's all your fault that I'm here. Get away from that, it's mine. Get away!' 'God, I hate rats,' thought Harry.

Then Harry had an idea. At first it seemed so horrible that he tried to push it away to the back of his mind, but it kept seeping through, until he had to accept that here lay his only chance.

His hand, stuck in the grill, was by now quite numb, and so, gritting his teeth, he began to rub it up and down against the mesh in which it was caught. His wrist was soon raw, and within ten minutes the blood had begun to flow – it seeped three inches down the iron to the water and then flowed off, leaving a small stain in the water directly in front of him. Harry felt in his pocket for a sodden box of matches. He pulled it out with his deformed arm and just managed to pitch it at the edge of the sewer, where the splash attracted the rats' attention. One by one they left the sack, and, noses gleaming and whiskers twitching, they slunk to the edge of the sewer. Harry grasped his trapped arm above the wrist, and held it as tightly as he could for a minute, then abruptly let go; there was a little spurt of blood. Immediately one of the rats lifted its head, stood poised for a second, then slithered over the edge and swam towards him. Harry closed his eyes and prayed. So far he could not actually feel anything, but he could hear the scrabbling of their claws against the ironwork. Then he felt a nip on one of his fingers – he almost yelled, but checked himself.

'Whatever happens,' he thought, 'I mustn't scare them off.' He felt another, and another, then a prolonged bite; he could feel the flesh being torn away, razor-sharp incisors meeting everywhere in his hand. The pain shot up Harry's arm in needle pricks, stabs, and long searing sheets of flame, as the little white teeth hungrily bit through his flesh into his muscle and bone.

Harry thought he was going mad. 'Christ Almighty, why didn't I settle for drowning – nothing could be worse than this.' Everything tumbled round in Harry's head, like a catherine-wheel in a biscuit tin; bright flashes of pain, the noise of the water, the cracking of bone and slobbering of flesh in tiny mouths, and Harry's own tortured murmurings.

Harry came to as he fell free of the grill, slipped into the water and was immediately swept up against it again. For a split second he wondered where he was, and then as it dawned on him, he pushed off from the grill with his legs, was carried to the side by the current and, heaving himself up on his elbows, scrambled out.

It was only when he stood up that he became conscious of the lack of sensation at the end of his good arm. He glanced down, his stomach heaved and he vomited violently. Where Harry, an hour ago, had had a hand, he now had the bloody mess of the palm of a hand, completely missing a thumb, and from which protruded the varying lengths of four finger stumps. The fleshy part of the hand had vanished, and on either side there was a tangle of sinew and muscle interspersed with fragments of bone.

Harry stood up again feeling weak at the knees. Turning his head away he thrust the sticky mess deep in his pocket, picked up the sack and set off, shuffling along the footpath. He had only gone fifty yards when his hand began to throb, and in five minutes it was on fire. Harry broke into a trot and eventually the long-awaited-for ladder and hatch materialized out of the gloom. He breathed a deep sigh of relief and even forgot the pain in his arm for a few seconds. 'Thank God,' he muttered, 'I made it.'

Pulling with the shrivelled claw of his malformed hand he heaved himself up the ladder, gripping the sack between his teeth as he went. Then he hitched the sack over the top rung and reached up for the handle of the manhole cover with his bad arm. Momentarily forgetting his wound, he pulled his other hand from his pocket, stretched up for the second handle and screamed as the cold metal met the raw flesh of his mutilated stump. He withdrew his hand, as from an electric shock and let it hang limp at his side. Then, gasping with pain he climbed one

rung higher and with
arm he shoved at the
Gritting his teeth he t
both hands, but the
consciousness.

Then Harry comple
the manhole cover wit
the side of the tunnel, a
rats,' he slithered dow
floor, just as the fainte
some distant sewer – the
water loosed by a sluice

ieces of Mary

Robert Ashley

y was rather a nice little girl really; that is until she got her
head chopped off. They had enjoyed doing that. Let me go
back just a bit; 'they' are the two quiet boys who lived next
door. On occasions they would play with Mary, since she didn't
have any real friends of her own. The other little girls in the
neighbourhood took a dislike to Mary and would poke fun at her.
Maybe this was due to the fact that Mummy would call Mary in
whenever she was seen with the other girls; Mummy thought
the other girls were naughty and definitely not the type that
Mary should associate herself with. They were a bad influence,
Mummy thought. Mind you, she was quite right; but Mary
didn't see it like that. However, it was all right for John and
David, the two little boys from next door, to come and play with
Mary; after all they were so quiet and good; altogether a good
influence.

John and David were rather inquisitive boys. Every toy they
had they pulled to pieces, just to see how it worked. Which
brings us to the question of Mary losing her head. The boys were
left rather dissatisfied after they had dissected their pet mouse.
There wasn't really enough to it. It didn't keep them occupied
for very long. They needed something a little bigger, a more
complex subject. Which again brings us to Mary; or rather it
brought them to Mary. For this is what they wanted their next
subject to be. What, they wondered, existed inside the head.
They had vague ideas after hearing about the brain and it being
the control point of the body. But what did it look like and how
did it work. Nobody had told them that. So they decided to find
out for themselves, and who would make the perfect subject,
who did they know best? Mary, of course.

It was Monday and they had two whole days off from school for half-term. This gave them plenty of time to get down to their studies. Most days they used the garden shed to play in, since this offered a fairly large space to move about in. They started by collecting together all the apparatus they were going to need: an old pair of kitchen scissors, a fairly sharp meat knife, several knitting needles of assorted sizes, and a small saw from their carpentry outfit. Now they were ready to call for Mary. They went and asked her if she'd like to come and play with them. She did, and went along with the boys to the shed thinking that there was some nice game that they could all play. And there was. John, being the eldest, picked up the knife and stuck it into Mary's throat. She didn't scream, but just stood still for a few moments before falling to the floor. David was delighted just to stand back and watch the blood pumping out of her body. John's shirt sleeve was covered in her blood as he was still standing close to Mary. David picked up the saw and handed it to John so that he could remove the head altogether; that would make the dissection a little easier, the rest of the body they could examine later. John placed the saw on Mary's neck near the point where the knife had entered and started to make a few cuts. It was a messy job as blood was still pouring out. He did his best and within a few minutes had sawn through about half the neck. Leaving the saw in position he let David take over for a while, after all he should share the fun as well. David continued the sawing with enthusiasm and after a few strokes the head gave a sudden move backwards. All the flesh had been cut away leaving the head suspended by the partly sawn through bone. John took over the sawing again after his rest. With a considerable effort he managed to cut completely through the bone so that the head rolled over a little, free from its body. David reached forward and picked up the head, moving it over to their workbench. A pool of blood accompanied his movement. Both wiped their hands to remove the sticky blood, looked at each other and smiled at their achievement. Now they could commence their investigation. David picked up a small knitting needle and prodded at the left eye. The eye moved about limply but he couldn't remove it. John came to his assistance with the scissors and cut around the eyelid. With a pair of knitting needles they managed to remove the eye from its socket. After making a cut through the connecting muscle the eye was removed altogether and placed in an aluminium tray to be kept at one side until later. Now they could set about their main task. Using the knife John made a cut across Mary's forehead; he had to make several cuts in order to go deep enough. David handed John a needle. Using this John was able to lift up the layers of skin so that he could insert the scissors and cut out a rectangular area. It was rather an untidy job; all that could be seen were the severed edges of skin and a part of the skull bone all awash with blood. John decided that much more cutting was necessary; this was going to be a longer job than at first thought. He cut away at the skin and hair on the top of Mary's head for nearly half an hour, removing several areas which were all placed in aluminium trays for future examination. By this time a fairly large area of the skull was exposed. They could now saw through the bone. John, being the stronger, picked up the saw and began scratching at the bone so as to ensure a good grip during the cutting. The actual sawing was hard work, but he managed to remove some of the bone. An area large enough for David to get his hand inside was exposed. First they looked inside to find out which bits they wanted, then David put his hand through the gap and probed about. He caught hold of one end of the brain and pulled it towards the outer edge of the hole so that they could cut off a piece and examine it properly. John made a clean slice through the organ since this was much easier to cut. They put the segment down on the table and examined it carefully, making several cuts in it to obtain more detail.

Just at that moment, when they were most absorbed with their work, they could hear their mother calling from the other end of the garden. It was time for lunch. They wiped the blood and bits from their hands as best they could and went towards the house. After lunch they could come back and look at the brain again and also at some of the other pieces of the head. They could even take out Mary's heart if there was enough time before tea. Daddy might like to see their work when he came home.

Miss Fletcher's Plum Tree

Frank Neate

The plums on Miss Fletcher's tree were exceedingly luscious. Plump and juicy, they hung pendulously in great quantities from the gnarled old limbs, tempting, mouth-watering, dark, glossy red skins almost bursting from the pressure of their delicious, incarnadined flesh. Dripping in veritable multitudes over Miss Fletcher's high stone wall from loaded boughs, these plums were a magnet to the little boys who played along the dusty road outside. Under the coolness of the profusion of leaves, branches and fruit many a local lad was wont to sit with his back to the wall, gobbling the ripe ones scattered below, aware, but youthfully uncaring, of the lazy summer scents hanging richly over the long, hot afternoons, and sometimes, in gangs, the boys came, to glut themselves on the windfalls first and then to piggy-back each other up to the less dusty and more tantalizing fruit still attached to the plum tree's branches. Occasionally, not too often to be sure, some more enterprising youngster would engineer a raid to the very top of the wall and, perhaps, in the secrecy of the foliage, to the heart of the tree itself, well inside the corner of Miss Fletcher's garden, there to sit quietly with the singlemindedness of a child, eating and eating, stones spraying with gentle plops to the dark, fibrous soil beneath.

Every year, this was the pattern. Sometimes Miss Fletcher caught the youngsters in the midst of their fruity feast. Often, a whole season would pass by with either fewer depredations or more skilful plum-raiders, and she would notice nothing unusual. When she did, she would shriek thinly, then chirrup at the children as they scampered nimbly back along the limbs and down to the road. 'You naughty, naughty children,' she would fuss. 'I'll tell your mothers. I know who you are. Oh, you rascals. If I catch you, you'll have to look out.' And like as not the children, from the safety of the road, would jeer, with the natural cruelty of little boys, at the angular, old-maidish figure, red-faced, fidgeting and upset behind the wall, 'Yah! silly ol' donkey Miss Fletcher,' or something similar. Perhaps inspired by the war it had once been 'silly ol' German', but that was long ago. And in any case, Miss Fletcher was not the slightest bit German. In fact, she was a second-generation New Zealander, and her ancestors were from the Old Country.

The boys were there now, five of them, impish and happy, creeping about the tree and gorging on ever more delectable plums, squealing softly when they found a particularly ripe sample, biting into the brimming flavour so that little rivulets of crimson juice ran down from the corners of their mouths and smeared pulpily over their chins with each successive morsel.

It was hot, almost brassy in the garden, and they revelled in the shade of their secret position ears nevertheless wary for the sounds of Miss Fletcher's birdlike movements as she pottered around in her loving-care sanctum. One kept watch from the sunny side of the tree but, as a sentry, he would inevitably have been shot eventually, for his thoughts ever strayed to the taste-bud paradise an arm's length away and he forgot to spy out the land for languid, gluttonish moments at a time.

Miss Fletcher was, of course, quite unaware of the raiders. The minute she knew she would flutter and fuss, but otherwise she would remain unaware of any loss for the tree was large and quite capable of accepting the annual pilferings from its copious supplies. There would be plums aplenty for Miss Fletcher, more than enough for her to rail to contemporary relatives, and from which to make jams and preserves for her own well-stocked larder and the little tête-a-têtes of the Country Women's Institute.

So she pottered in her garden, cutting at the trim edges of her cool, green lawns, plastic-gloved hands firmly grasping secateurs to snip away an unsightly twig from the standard roses, hoe moving rhythmically in the shrubbery, hand fork savagely routing some daring weed from her precious flowerbeds.

It was warm and relaxing in the garden for Miss Fletcher. She enjoyed her never-ending pottering. On a little foam-rubber mat she knelt here and there, floppy linen hat shading her face and neck, pausing periodically to wipe the faint blur of sweat from her spectacles. Miss Fletcher was invariably happy in her garden. She enjoyed the feel of the well-manured soil, abhorred untidiness. Each section of her domain was as perfect as her hands could make it, flowers arranged in order of size and colour, shrubs and trees planted decorously, even a corner with delicate miniature native ferns and a few bigger *pongas* fanning restfully above, their rust-coloured dead fronds drifting gently down the notched, dark fibrous trunks from the vigorous dark-green tracery of new and abundant crown growth. This was Miss Fletcher's routine, a pleasing way of life even if lonely, for apart from her occasional attendance at Institute functions, Miss Fletcher much preferred to be by herself.

She was no recluse, but her excursions outside her own section were infrequent. Her few bills were paid by cheque, and local trades people in the nearby country town delivered her requirements as she telephoned for them. Miss Fletcher was far from extravagant, but she obviously did not lack for money. She had not worked for years, if she had ever worked at all, so the people round about assumed, quite correctly, that she had independent means.

Yet perhaps the very solitude of years was not really good for Miss Fletcher.

She tended to become most irritable about trivials, adopted a slightly unrealistic and, at times, uncharitable attitude if there was any odd ruffle on the surface of her generally placid, rustic existence – like stores from the grocer's arriving late, her newspaper flung into a puddle instead of being placed snugly in the short galvanized-iron pipe section by her neat letterbox, people glancing quite naturally but, to her mind, slyly in her direction on her odd visits to town. And lately, she had been talking to herself in a friendly, chatty sort of way, blissfully unaware there was anything strange in this.

Miss Fletcher, then, finished parting some carnations and straightened her thin back with a sigh. The heat was becoming a little uncomfortable and there were sweaty stains under the armpits of her blue gardening dress. She rose stiffly and glanced around pridefully at her most attractive garden, almost screened from the road by the mellowed stone front wall and white-painted paling gate. Somewhere, a black and yellow bee, legs gigantic and orange with waxy pollen, bumbled among the flowers, a fantail twittered and darted in the fernery, and the sound of the cicadas was heavy and enchanting on the summer stillness.

Slowly, Miss Fletcher minced along, a little weary from the kneeling and the heat, but sprightly, nevertheless, for her years, which no one knew exactly, but which must have been around the sixty-mark for she had once let slip that she was born about the turn of the century.

'My word,' she said lightly to herself. 'My word, you've done a good job here. Anita' – for that was her Christian name – 'you've made this garden into a picture. You should enter the "Beautiful Garden" contest.' And she giggled girlishly, then snorted, 'Silly old thing you are. There aren't any "Beautiful Garden" contests in the country. You have to go to a big city to enter those.' And she bubbled over again. 'Imagine me in a big city, though!' The thought was too, too absurd.

Then Miss Fletcher saw a stone on the lawn and instantly her mood changed. At once she was pettish and annoyed. 'Those boys again. Those little rascals. I'll bet they've been throwing stones on the roof again. Oh! what I wouldn't do to them if I caught them.' And she smiled suddenly, a sly, funny little smile, at the surprising thought.

Away went the stone over the wall and she drew near to the plum tree, head cocked on one side rather like a fussy and scrawny chicken. Somewhere a *tui* jangled its unusual call, and up ahead there was a rustling in the leafy closeness of the tree. Miss Fletcher saw it and hopped forward briskly.

'Pss-sst, beat it you kids. The ol' girl's on the warpath,' came in a stage whisper from the tree and there was an immediate frantic bustling and a shaking. Plums dropped with dull thuds and twigs crackled as the five raiders crept hastily to the freedom of the road.

Miss Fletcher ran in under the tree to its mossy bole, peered up into the dappled greenness and a plum dropped squashily on to the crown of her hat. She wrung her gardening gloves together then scrabbled high in the air as though to stop the marauders with her clutching fingertips.

'Oh, you rascals,' she squealed. 'Oh, you little rascals. I'll tell your mothers. I'll tell the schoolmaster. You little thieves. Just wait till I catch you.'

But the birds had flown. Miss Fletcher ceased waving her arms as the last grey shirt slipped out of sight behind the wall, brown young arms confidently releasing their hold on the sturdy branch.

And when she stood on a box to look over the wall, they were racing down the macadam road as fast as their feet would take them, one or two plums flipping out from overstuffed shirt-fronts. They all turned around at the corner, success in a mission accomplished overcoming alarm, and laughed merrily at the ridiculous, spectacled face in the floppy hat peering angrily over the wall at them. One little chap of about eight or nine almost put his fingers to his nose in an obscene gesture, but apparently thought better of it and contented himself with a high 'Ha! Ha!' before picking up his heels and taking off after his cobbers.

Miss Fletcher stood by the wall for a long, long time, shaking and livid with frustrated anger. Gradually, she calmed down and soon felt well enough to go back to the house. Unaccountably though, she had an overwhelming inclination to stay, but she first moved her box to a position from which she could see over the wall but not be seen.

About half an hour later, she saw a boy come ambling around the corner, scuffling his gumboots in the dust and mooching – that was the only word for it – vaguely towards the bush and the paddocks nearer the river beyond her place. It was the boy who had laughed and run after the others. She watched him avidly as he passed, the scent of plums strong in her nostrils, leaves brushing her hat.

And that was when the Voice came, quite clearly, seeming to reverberate in her head with its precise enunciation.

'There is a solution to these little rascals you know, Anita, and particularly to this little thief. It's so perfectly feasible, and really quite simple. Don't you see, this is how you tackle it . . .'

And in those quiet, listening moments, Miss Fletcher went quite queer.

The boy glanced warily at the wall as he passed, decided everything was fine, and began skipping on his way to do what boys do on hot summer afternoons. The plum stains were dirty on his chin and upper lip. Miss Fletcher hardly noticed as he disappeared out of sight. She was standing quite still, listening, and all the upsets of the stolen plums and the people staring slyly at her dissipated, drawn gently from her mind and thrust away into the humid air as new and startling thoughts took their place.

There was purpose in her brisk strides as she moved suddenly from her box and went towards her white, weatherboard home.

Inside, she stripped off her gardening gloves and placed them neatly on the kitchen bench, then rummaged for a few minutes in a cupboard containing suitcases, old shoes, and the miscellaneous accumulations of years. She stepped into her spare bedroom and carefully laid about half a dozen thin leather straps on the single bed. Then she took an old coat, laid it over the back of a chair in the kitchen, and meticulously set a stool at the table.

Then Miss Fletcher began humming brightly to herself, no longer in the least bit querulous, and set about making a nice hot cup of tea.

The boy was just the ordinary, common-garden variety, straight hair, mischievous hazel eyes, snub nose splashed faintly with freckles, and peeling a little from the sun, and pursed lips now whistling loudly and off-key some vaguely familiar air. His grey flannel shirt had the tail flapping over grey shorts, and his scout belt was all askew because it was pushed through two or three loops only.

His gumboots scuffed inevitably in the dust as he walked

back along the road to Miss Fletcher's place, both grimy hands cupped lovingly around his prize, a dry, glossy-skinned lizard with bright, black beady eyes.

The shadows were lengthening a little as he trudged along, and even the cicadas were reducing the noise level of their summery sounds. Over the fences came the lowing of cows moving towards the milking sheds, hooves thumping on the worn, sun-baked bush tracks.

For the boy, the plum raid was old hat, something that had occurred aeons ago. Thus there was no real disquiet now as he moved steadily along past Miss Fletcher's wall. But he did start when a tinkling laugh sounded in his right ear as he came, head down, beside her paling gate.

'Hello, little man. Would you like a nice piece of cake on such a fine, hot afternoon?'

And there she was, smiling languidly, glasses on her beaky nose glinting in the sunlight. The floppy hat was gone and so were the gardening gloves, but otherwise it was the same old Miss Fletcher who had called out in anger to them earlier on, and the boy was automatically wary. He stopped and eyed her, muscles alert for the quick getaway, but content to listen to any reasonable proposition.

'Yes,' she repeated, still smiling as enticingly as she could, 'a lovely piece of sponge cake, with whipped cream in the middle and icing on the top.'

The boy was sorely tempted, but past experience had shown it did not pay to acquiesce too readily to adult suggestions.

'Can't,' he said.

'Why ever not?' asked Miss Fletcher in a high voice, a little shadow of anxiety flickering across her thin face.

''Cause,' said the boy.

'Because what?' said Miss Fletcher. 'Not just a teeny weeny piece of lovely sponge cake?'

'What about my lizard?' the boy demanded gruffly.

'Oh,' said Miss Fletcher, relief chasing the peculiar anxiety from her face, 'he can come right in with you as well and we'll see if we can find a jamjar to put him in.'

She opened the gate and beckoned the boy in.

He hesitated, looked along the road, then decided the cake was too good to miss and marched in.

'Mum'll wonder where I am if I don't get home soon,' he said.

'A piece of cake will only take you a minute,' smiled Miss Fletcher. 'Now come along,' and she shepherded him down the neat, concrete path between the red and white standard roses, up the steps and on to the veranda, then through the cool passage to her tidy little kitchen.

'Well, here we are,' she said briskly. 'Now let's see about this sponge cake. You sit up at the table on that stool and I'll have a look in my tins. I've such a lot of nice things for good little boys here.'

She bustled about and placed a thick slice of cake on a plate in front of the youngster. 'There now, eat it all up. We must do this more often.'

'What about my lizard?' said the boy, unmoving.

'Oh yes. How silly of me,' said Miss Fletcher. 'Now where did I see a clean jamjar . . . ah yes, here we are, and there's even a top for it. Have to put a few holes in that, won't we, so that your lizard can breathe nicely?'

She punched a few holes in the lid with a tin opener and placed the jar beside the sponge cake on the table.

The boy put the lizard inside, put the top on loosely, and munched into his cake as he watched his prize, motionless except for the flickering tongue and bright, swivelling eyes, lying on the round glass at the bottom.

Miss Fletcher hummed merrily and bustled around the kitchen for a moment, then she walked back through the house and out to the gate where she looked carefully up and down the road. There was no one in sight, and apart from a sudden fast-flipping flight of goldfinches, their yellow and black wings flashing over the gorse bushes on the other side of the road, she saw no living thing.

Back in the house, the boy was on the last lap of his sponge cake. He turned as Miss Fletcher came in but she beamed at him again and he soon went back to his munching and a steady watch on the lizard in its glass prison.

Miss Fletcher breathed a little faster, tension rising in her. She poised herself, savouring the movement, then she swooped with a speed that was surprising. One moment the old coat was over the back of the chair, the next it was dropped securely over the boy's head and upper body, enveloping and pinioning his arms, and she was half carrying half dragging him to the spare bedroom, chuckling heartily, victoriously, as he kicked his legs. Excitement danced in Miss Fletcher's eyes.

The lizard bottle was knocked to the floor in the slight scuffle. The lid came off and the tiny creature inside slipped like a shadow to the nearest sanctuary, body and tail writhing as his belly slid over the slippery linoleum.

In the bedroom, Miss Fletcher dumped her heaving, squirming bundle on the bed, face flushing as she grabbed for one of the straps. The boy was like an eel and he started to yell but she held the coat tightly around him with one hand and, dropping the strap, soundly cuffed him where she supposed his ears to be. He stopped wriggling a little and began a muffled angry weeping.

The boy was a little toughie but Miss Fletcher's hands and arms were quite strong. And in this moment, she felt a warming excess of power. Quickly she pulled the boy's hands and arms from under the voluminous coat and with a few deft, economical movements born of twining and tying in her garden, strapped them tightly together in front of him. She worked tirelessly and used up all the straps, binding him tightly until he lay trussed and frightened on the green counterpane.

Then she pulled the coat from his head, smacked his cheeks hard for good measure, and produced a long scarf with which she gagged his mouth tightly so that nothing more than a muffled murmuring and the tears trickling down the side of his hot cheeks indicated he was crying his heart out.

Miss Fletcher stepped back from the bed and looked at the strapped-up figure. She was panting, and a few wisps of hair straggled down over her reddened face. She licked thin lips then smiled again broadly to show a mouthful of china-white dentures. 'Ho hum,' she said. 'Well now, that's done quite satisfactorily, thank you. What a naughty little rascal you are. But I've got you now. Naughty boys must be punished . . .

punished quite severely, and we know what to do with you now, don't we? Fancy taking all poor Miss Fletcher's plums. That sort of thing can't go unpunished now, can it?'

And she sat on the bed beside him in an abrupt movement and began alternately slapping his face and twisting his ears until his eyes screwed up and the portion of face visible above the gag contorted with the pain. She cuffed him again and again, rubbed his scalp hard, and pinched his legs and arms.

'Such a naughty boy,' she squealed, quite happily, 'we'll have to fix him, won't we, Anita? We've got to be cruel to be kind. A little discipline seems to be required.'

And the boy quivered in terror, straining in the straps as her laughing, spectacled eyes loomed above his, long, wispy grey hair brushing his face, and hands kneading, pummelling, pinching and slapping his body in joyous abandon.

Miss Fletcher's house was like many old homes in New Zealand, weatherboard on timber framing, scrimmed, papered inside walls, iron roof, rambling, with old sash-type windows and the inevitable front veranda. But it had one unusual difference. There was a cellar. Miss Fletcher had used it for years for storing unwanted items and for keeping her vegetables, preserves and other odds and ends. It was dry with a concrete, linoleum-covered floor and a long, frosted-glass window just above ground level which let in adequate daylight. The cellar was reached by a small door in the hall, leading down a flight of wooden steps.

It was down there that Miss Fletcher took her prisoner – she already thought of him as such – as soon as she had tired of making him quake and squirm. This was not for some time because the punishment she inflicted gave her a warm, delicious feeling of contentment, almost exhilaration.

Finally though, she placed her strong arms and hands under him, and carried him out into the passage and down the steps.

It was cool in the cellar with the smell of old leather and kapok, the sourish tang of cabbages, and the pungent aroma of floor polish and disinfectant merging with that of dust and concrete and borer-ridden match-lining walls.

Miss Fletcher laid the boy bruisingly on the floor in her haste, then hunted among pieces of furniture and Victorian knick-knacks for an old single-bed mattress she had placed there months before. She found it and dragged it out to the middle of the floor and plunked the boy on top of it.

'There we are, mustn't let you get cold and damp, must we?' she said. 'I'm hoping this little boy, this naughty little boy, will be with me for quite some time so I can teach him some manners.' She paused reflectively. 'Cold ... cold, yes that's it, of course. Blankets, that's what we want.' And she darted bird-like up the stairs to reappear a moment later with three or four blankets which she tucked carefully around the bound boy.

'There we are, all tucked up for the night,' she chuckled. 'Don't you look funny. Mustn't glare like that or I might have to cover your eyes up too, mightn't I?'

There was a rending, choked sob from behind the scarf, and the boy's eyes were brimming with tears again.

'Oh, poor little boy,' said Miss Fletcher, and she dashed out again to reappear a second later. 'Perhaps he's cold around the head.' Swiftly she pulled an old red woollen balaclava over his head and outside the gag.

The boy lay there looking ridiculous.

'Ho hum,' said Miss Fletcher again, smiled benignly and marched up the stairs.

The boy, hot and prickly in the tickling woollen helmet, heard the key turn in the lock before he surrendered to a new fit of sobbing in the semi-gloom of the cellar.

Miss Fletcher had thoroughly enjoyed her tea. She seemed to have a new-found sense of taste as she nibbled greedily at succulent lamb's fry and tender vegetables from her own garden. A drenching summer rain began as she finished the washing up, and it carried the dust from the leaves and petals, giving new enchantment to the abundant flora around the house.

The rain was so welcome, in fact, that Miss Fletcher went out in it. She stood on the lawn and let it soak her blue dress, delightedly felt its caressing rivulets streaming off her hair and

down the back of her neck. The glass of her spectacles was running with raindrops and she stared deliciously up at the black
clouds, then through the blur at her colourful borders and plots
and greenery.

'Ho, ho,' she laughed. 'What a delight when you're waterproof.
Let it rain, let it pour, I'll be waterproof for ever more.' And
she sang the words over and over again in a high-pitched little
melody.

But the rain stopped eventually and there was the gorgeous
noise all round her of water soaking and gurgling into the soil,
dripping from leaf to branch and from branch to petal, coursing
down the tree trunks and beading the fern fronds, glinting like
diamond droplets in the folds of rich-textured roses.

So Miss Fletcher went inside as the twilight came, disdainful
of her sopping dress and straggling hair, there to make herself
a nice hot cup of tea.

She heard the front gate click about an hour later, and then
the hesitant knock on the front door.

'Oh, excuse me,' said the pretty young woman. 'You're Miss
Fletcher, aren't you?' She looked anxious in the glow of Miss
Fletcher's veranda light.

Miss Fletcher smiled kindly at her.

'I'm Mrs Reeves . . . from farther down the road. I wonder –
I wonder if you've seen a little boy passing here at all. It's my
Ian actually. He took off somewhere this afternoon and it's
getting so late I'm beginning to get a bit anxious. He's usually
home well before this. He's only just on nine.'

'Oh you poor thing,' said Miss Fletcher solicitously. 'But I
wouldn't worry too much. I expect he'll be back before long.
They usually come home when they're hungry if *I know* little
boys. But really, I wouldn't know if I've seen him or not. I see
a lot of little boys around here and I can't really tell one from
another. I did see a boy going past here up towards the river
about four o'clock, but I'm afraid beyond that I can't be much
help. I'll certainly keep my eyes open though.' She smiled
kindly again. 'You look quite worried. What about my making
you a nice cup of tea?'

'Well, I really think I ought to have a look farther on,' said the young woman. 'His father should be home soon. He had to go to town today.'

'Nonsense,' said Miss Fletcher firmly. 'No sense in wearing yourself out. Come on inside.' And she placed her hand on the young woman's arm and steered her firmly down the passage and into the kitchen.

As she made the tea, chattering busily all the while, the young woman noticed her damp dress.

'You've been caught in the shower,' she said. 'I think I'd change into a dry frock if I were you. You might catch a cold.'

Miss Fletcher stopped bustling, surprised. 'Why it never worries me,' she said. 'You see, I'm waterproof.'

What an odd time to make jokes. I suppose she's just trying to cheer me up, thought the young woman, although how serious she seemed. Ah well, perhaps she's one of these dry old maids.

They drank their tea and pretty soon the young woman said she'd have to go.

'I do hope your little boy is all right,' said Miss Fletcher as she saw her guest out the front door. 'But I expect he'll be home when you get there.'

'I hope so,' sighed the young woman.

The faint cry, high, muffled and anguished, came as she turned to go. She stiffened. 'Whatever's that?' she whispered.

Consternation streaked across Miss Fletcher's face. 'Oh dearie me,' she said. 'I'll have to leave you. It's my cat, Whiskers. Sounds as though he's shut in the cellar. That's the second time this week.' And she rushed off down the passage as the worried mother hesitated, then shrugged and walked along the concrete path, clicked open the paling gate, and stepped out into the dampened road.

At eleven o'clock Miss Fletcher was busily sewing. She was a good needlewoman and her hands worked nimbly on a strange garment adapted from a large, clean sack. At the bottom, she had cut holes and neatly bound the openings with linen strips. At the top, left open, she had double sewn a long piece of stiffened material to stop the sack from fraying and to give it added strength. Then she had securely sewn on two long, strong leather loops to front and back so that the whole looked like a rather gargantuan, elongated shopping bag with openings at the bottom.

She was a little weary from all the excitement when she finished and was just about to prepare for bed when there was a knock at the front door, not hesitant this time, rather determined, officious.

'Good evening,' said the policeman. 'I'm Constable Johnson. I don't suppose you happened to see a small boy anywhere about here this afternoon, did you?'

'Oh dear, Mrs Reeves' little Ian hasn't come home yet,' said Miss Fletcher.

'Oh,' said the constable, 'then you *have* seen him.'

'Oh dear no,' said Miss Fletcher. 'At least, I may have, but all little boys are much the same to me. You see such a lot of them playing around here. No, you see Mrs Reeves did ask me the same question earlier this evening. Dear me, what a shame. She was *so* distressed.'

'Oh,' said the constable again; then, 'I see. That's all right then. Just thought you might have been able to help. You see he hasn't come home and we're inquiring at all the houses around here. Looks as though it'll be an all-night session. We've got a search party starting off in half an hour or so. Hope the little bloke hasn't met with an accident.'

'The river,' said Miss Fletcher, horrified. 'I wonder . . .' Her voice trailed off as the policeman looked grim.

'Let's sincerely hope not,' he said. Then briskly, 'Well, thanks Miss Fletcher. I'll be getting along.'

'Goodnight,' she called as his heavy boots clumped down the path.

Inside, with the door bolted for the night once more, Miss Fletcher's face wore a smug, secretive smile. 'Oh, what a one you are, Anita,' she said to herself.

She was still humming as she pressed her hair-netted, creamed face into the pillow and fell soundly asleep.

It was another beautiful sunny day when Miss Fletcher stretched and awoke. Only a soloist in the cicada world had begun his daily chore, but already the air was filled with bird noises and sheep baa-aaed in the distance.

Languidly, with restrained excitement, Miss Fletcher arose in her long pink nightie, stripped off the hair net and made for her pastel-painted bathroom. She pursued her toilet intently and meticulously. A lovely hot bath with plenty of bath salts and bubbles, the glorious luxury of warm water over her flat stomach and withered breasts, then the brisk towelling and clean under-wear. Then the girdle, petticoat, most frilly, and her new print frock slipped on last.

In big, furry slippers she padded into the kitchen and pre-pared her breakfast. She sang *Cruising Down the River* as she washed up. Then it was a brisk, deep-breathing stroll around the garden, during which she nodded to several weary-looking men in working clothes and gumboots who passed her gate from the direction of the river.

'No luck,' said one.

'Oh, I *am* sorry,' said Miss Fletcher. 'What a terrible thing for the mother. Poor little mite.'

The men refused her kind offer of a cup of tea, saying every-thing was laid on at a hall in the township. Soon they disappeared down the road, already dusty in spite of the previous evening's shower, and Miss Fletcher flitted inside with another little smile of anticipation.

She primped and preened in front of her huge dressing-table mirror, perched on the exquisitely-padded stool as she care-fully arranged her greying hair. She applied a little discreet make-up, drew on her best black gloves, slipped on neat, low-heeled black shoes, and lastly, set a summer cloche hat in white with pink flowers on her head and stepped briskly to the kitchen. The excitement in her was intense now. She placed the sacking device over one arm, picked up a bowl of porridge in one hand, and went out in the hall to the cellar door, which she unlocked.

As an afterthought, she went to a cupboard and plucked out a thin, whippy cane. Then gripping it firmly, she walked down the stairs.

The boy was awake and still frightened. The gag was firmly in place. Her adjustment after the 'Whiskers' episode of the night before had been too much for him.

Carefully, Miss Fletcher set her things down on a box and went over to him. 'Well,' she said, 'what a beautiful morning. I hope you had a good night's sleep. We're going to start our lessons in good manners and discipline today. Little boys who steal plums must be cured, and I'm going to cure you with good, old-fashioned punishment and kindness. Now, let's have this off, but you had better not make a noise if you know what's good for you.'

The boy's face was red and marked from the gag when she took it off, and he gasped as though he were breathing air through his mouth for the first time in his life. He looked as though he was going to cry again, but something in Miss Fletcher's benign countenance must have deterred him.

'Now then, let's have some breakfast first. Like some breakfast?'

The boy said nothing. He glared warily at his tormentor above him.

'What's this? Cat got your tongue?' And Miss Fletcher smacked his face lightly. 'Now answer when you're spoken to. Would you like some breakfast?'

The boy all but dissolved into tears again, but he managed to blurt out one word – 'No.'

'Oh,' said Miss Fletcher, 'you'd better have some all the same.' And she sat him up, balaclava and all, and proceeded to feed him cold porridge with a spoon. Though he gagged and spluttered, once showering her frock front with a saliva-filled mouthful, she shovelled the stuff into him with energetic purpose.

'That's that,' she said at last. 'And now I'm going to punish you for stealing. When I was a little girl, our teacher used to give us the cane when we were naughty and that's what we're going to give you, you naughty little tyke you.' She shuddered impatiently as her fingers scrabbled at the straps fastening his legs.

Then she pushed and prodded him into the sacklike garment, his arms and hands still firmly trussed, until his legs projected through the holes at the bottom. His gumboots and socks she removed.

From the ceiling of Miss Fletcher's cellar a pulley arrangement was suspended. What its original purpose had been was hard to say, but Miss Fletcher put it to use now for the first time in years. She tied a strong rope to the leather loops at the top of the bag containing the boy, pushed the end through the pulley and, exerting all her strength, hauled bag and boy up until they were suspended about three feet off the floor. The boy looked even more ridiculous and helpless and he swung gently, just his legs and balaclava-covered head showing and the tears already starting from frightened eyes again.

'There we are,' said Miss Fletcher, smiling broadly. 'We're almost ready now.' She tied the cord's end to a convenient outsize hook on the wall and skipped over to pick up the cane.

It was swishing, and horrible in the boy's ears.

'Here goes,' shouted Miss Fletcher, swinging it swooshingly through the air. The first stinging blow brought a wild yelp from the boy.

Miss Fletcher stopped, annoyed. 'Oh dear, we can't have that noise,' she said, and gagged him with the scarf again.

Then she began caning him in earnest, great smarting whacks on the buttocks swinging gently in their sacking cradle. She flailed the cane again and again until she was hot and breathless. She danced around him as she caned and, to make this easier, slipped off her shoes. The flowers on her hat flip-flopped as she darted around him, and she squealed in ecstatic enjoyment, the smile remaining throughout.

'Oh, it's nice to be waterproof,' she sang as she thrashed him. 'This is the way we teach naughty boys who steal plums, isn't it,' she trilled, and in time to it all, the thwack and swish of the cane.

At last, she was spent and she threw the cane down. The boy swung slumped in his bag, his eyes closed, face pallid.

'Perhaps he's fainted. They were tougher when I was young', said Miss Fletcher as she trudged slowly up the stairs.

The garden was bright and the air fresh with a faint zephyr when she walked out. The plums hung as luscious as ever on the tree in the corner, and there were many bees droning here and there. On the road, there was quite a bit of traffic, mainly cars filled with frowning men.

Miss Fletcher pottered in the garden, snipping here, plucking there, did all her housework, arranged fresh roses in her sitting-room, and at lunchtime and dinnertime descended into the cellar for further sessions with the boy.

She fed him with porridge each time, caned him with gay abandon, yet assiduously, delivered an extra thrashing when he fouled the bag, then relented, lowered him to the floor, plucked him from the sack, and assisted him to make use of a bucket in a dark corner of the cellar.

That night, she tucked the blankets around his still-firmly-trussed body, then went up to telephone her grocer.

'Reckon the old girl must be getting a sweet tooth in her old age,' that slightly bewildered young man told his wife later. 'She wants two big ice-cream packs, a big box of chocolates, a dozen packets of assorted sweet biscuits and a whole swag of lollies – oh, and bottles of fizzy drinks.'

'Oh well,' said his wife practically, 'it has been terribly hot, and anyway – who cares? More turnover for us and goodness knows we need it if we're going to see the All Blacks in Australia.'

Miss Fletcher was attentive to her toilet the next morning, but she did not dress up as though for a trip to town, contenting herself with the now-washed and pressed blue gardening frock. She took her usual stroll around the garden and said 'Hello' to the policeman cycling past.

He stopped beside her gate and shrugged his shoulders significantly. 'Looks bad,' he said. 'We're dragging what parts of the river we can today and patrolling the banks where we can't. But she's a mighty deep river in places. Doesn't look too hopeful to me. The boy's mother is frantic. She had a proper break-down last night and they took her to hospital. The father looks as though he hasn't slept for a week. It's terrible to see it. Poor little chap! Pity boys are always so adventurous, isn't it? He was a friendly little joker, too. Always used to say "Good day" to me, and all the people round here seemed to like him.'

'What a *shame*,' said Miss Fletcher, unctuously emphasizing the last word. 'What a perfectly terrible thing to happen around here. Isn't there any chance at all?'

'Don't think so,' said the constable despondently. "Course, he *could* be lost up in the bush, but I very much doubt it. We found his pocket-knife down near the river. That looks about it.'

'I wonder,' said Miss Fletcher hesitantly, 'I wonder if I could help at all, getting on though I am. Perhaps I could help look after the other children at home now that Mrs Reeves is in hospital.'

'Very nice of you,' said the policeman, 'but I think everything is well taken care of. If we don't find him by the morning I think we'll have done about all we can. Well, must be off. Hooray, Miss Fletcher.'

'Goodbye,' she called as he pedalled off along the road.

She was just about to go inside when the grocer arrived in his van.

''Morning Miss Fletcher. Here's your order. Wanted some ice-cream to cool off in this weather, did you?'

'I just decided to treat myself,' said Miss Fletcher coquettishly. 'Aren't I an old silly?'

'Not a bit of it,' said the grocer. 'Do you good.' He stopped, became serious. 'Terrible about young Ian Reeves isn't it?'

'Just awful,' said Miss Fletcher. 'Too terrible for words. His poor mother.'

Back in the house, she arranged many things on a tray and went down to the cellar. 'Well, and how's my boy this morning? All set for another lesson?' she chirruped brightly.

The boy's eyes blinked and he flickered them towards the cane on the floor.

'Oh no,' said Miss Fletcher. 'Today is Kindness Day. That's part of the therapy. No caning today – unless of course you're not nice.'

She took the gag from the boy's mouth, removed the blankets and unstrapped his limbs, first fixing a broad belt around his waist to which she attached a long length of dog chain at the small of the back. This, in turn, she secured to a hook high in the wall.

The boy was in agony as his circulation came back. For long moments he lay there, unable to stand up and, when he did, she had to help him as he eased small, cramped arms, wrists and legs.

Miss Fletcher picked up the cane and he flinched in terror. She swished it wickedly as an example of what could be in store, then said: 'Now be good, and make absolutely no noise. If you shout or speak when you're not spoken to, I'll have to strap you up again and give you another good thrashing. You wouldn't like that, would you?'

'No,' gulped the boy, then he sobbed out, heart-rending, 'I want my mummy.'

'Now,' said Miss Fletcher sternly, and lifted the cane.

The boy choked back his tears and was silent.

After that, she rubbed salve on his welts, sat him down tenderly on a chair, and plied him with fruit, lollies and ice-cream, forcing him to eat when he showed signs of losing interest. Once, he looked hopelessly at the window and the door, but Miss Fletcher had only to gesture towards the cane and that was that.

At intervals that day she fed him on rich, delicious dishes, even delectable ripe plums from the tree in the corner of her garden. All the time she spent with him she chattered gaily of this and that, regaled him with tales of her girlhood, and even provided him with long-forgotten jokes and riddles of another era. She made him play simple games and kept on pushing him to eat whatever he fancied. He was sick after one session and, after cleaning up the mess, she whacked him a couple of times with the cane – but not very hard.

And throughout that long day, he spoke only when spoken to, valiantly, but in fear, held back most of his ready tears, and not once attempted to cry out for help.

At night, she took off the belt and chain, strapped him up and gagged him again. Then she tucked him up, cowering, into his mattress.

The full-scale search ended on the afternoon of the next day as Miss Fletcher learned from a neighbour going past.

As the man walked away, he wondered whether Miss Fletcher had just come back from town or whether she was just going out, for she was dressed up, wild-rice summer coat, high, shapeless hat, white gloves and shoes.

But Miss Fletcher had neither been, nor was going, anywhere.

The routine of 'lessons' continued in the cellar for three sessions during the day – cold porridge and thrashings, with the only relief for the boy infrequent spells out of the suspended bag and at the bucket in the corner.

So it went on for almost a fortnight – Kindness Days, Punishment Days, each one a time for delicious excitement or warm contentment for Miss Fletcher.

But the time came when she realized her new activities meant she was neglecting her garden, and this was brought home forcibly to her one day when she saw dozens of ripe plums rotting under the tree in the corner of the garden.

'Ho hum, something will have to be done,' she said. 'But we can't send naughty boys home to their mothers, however much they're wanted, can we, Anita?'

And as before, she stood quiet, almost rigid, when the Voice shrilled insistently inside her head.

'But of course you can't send him home, Anita. That would never do. But there *is* a solution, you know. Mind you, you'll have to wrap him up well, for it might be cold and damp. But he'll be safe there, and he'll be quiet and polite. Now, here's what you must do . . .'

Miss Fletcher walked purposefully back to the house and made a phone call. Then she went quietly down to the cellar and tenderly, solicitously, fed the boy a huge plate of strawberry ice-cream . . . for it was Kindness Day.

'Buckets she wants now,' said the grocer to his wife. 'Perhaps she'll be filling them with ice-cream.'

'She wants to fill them up with something,' said his wife smoothly, 'but I'll bet it's not ice-cream!'

How right she was.

There was a gusty wind with a hint of rain that night when

Miss Fletcher took the boy for a walk. And there was no moon.

Gently, she pushed the boy in front of her down the back garden path, through the bush track and on down to the wide, sluggish river which curled back in and ran not far from the rear of her home.

The boy stumbled along, the scarf around his mouth and his arms secured tightly. Miss Fletcher carried the two buckets, more straps, a length of rope, and an old, rubberized raincoat over one arm.

It was chilly down by the swirling water, but she took off the boy's gumboots and socks. Then she stood him up in the buckets and strapped each leg firmly to the handles. She also tied the rope tightly to the handles and then up around his shoulders and on to the straps trussing his arms.

'You won't be cold or wet, anyway. That's one blessing,' she said to the boy whose eyes screamed silently and unseen in the darkness. 'I'll put this coat round you.'

She did so, buttoning and belting it carefully and tightly. She bent down to his face. 'What a pity you're not waterproof, like me,' she confided.

Then, lastly Miss Fletcher filled the buckets with gravel and large stones, placing them carefully so she would not hurt the boy's feet as she buried them.

'I'll be sorry to see you go,' said Miss Fletcher. 'We've had such happy times, such fun together, and I think I've taught you not to be naughty and a thief. But I'm so busy and my work is being neglected. I just haven't the time any longer.' And, to herself, 'Anyway, Anita, perhaps next year, who knows?'

She grabbed the boy around the body and pulled him to the riverbank. It was agonizingly difficult with the weights on his feet, but she managed it at last.

She patted him on the head, then forced the buckets off the steep bank almost simultaneously, and the strangely-clad figure shot like a plum-bob into the deep, deep darkness of the water. The last Miss Fletcher saw of the boy was a fleeting glimpse of his woollen balaclava. Then a few bubbles shot to the surface to be swiftly obliterated in the oily current. Then the river was swirling past, unruffled by anything save the elements.

'Ho hum,' said Miss Fletcher, 'and that's that,' as she walked back through the gusty night, her boots squelching in a swampy piece of ground.

And summer changed to the russet and burnt orange of autumn, and the plums under Miss Fletcher's tree rotted and were covered by falling leaves, there to remain, changing to rich mould, their fertility ready to help the burgeoning sap to begin its annual climb in the spring, and give glowing life to the delicate blossoms and setting fruit.

Deep down in the river, in the muddy gravel and snags of years, a horror floated from two weighted buckets like some shadowy push-down-spring-up-again doll. And the eels and the trout and the myriad water creatures – some microscopic but horrific in shape – with claw and mouth and sucker and tentacle, fed well through the autumn, long winter and spring from the nameless alien in their company.

And time helped to assuage a mother's grief, but did no more than patch her broken heart.

Then the summer came in all its splendour and the plums on Miss Fletcher's tree were luscious and red once more – plenty luscious for small boys to raid on the long, hot afternoons after school was out.

They sat there now, gorging on ever more delectable fruit, squealing softly when they found a particularly ripe sample, biting into the brimming flavour so that little rivulets of crimson juice ran down the corners of their mouths and smeared pulpily over their chins with each successive morsel.

The sentry was most lax. Suddenly, in the act of sinking his teeth into a juicy plum, he became aware of Miss Fletcher standing below and looking fixedly up at him, plastic-gloved hands clasped decorously in front of her. The boy didn't much like her look.

'Scram you kids,' he squeaked, and they all scrambled away like mad along the limbs, dropped off into the road and took to their heels without looking back.

A speculative look came into Miss Fletcher's eyes as she peered over the wall after them. She stood silent for long moments, then strode briskly back into her white, weatherboard home, there to make certain arrangements.

And a sly, secretive smile flickered on her thin face.

The Nursery Club

Martin Ricketts

When I first arrived at Brandon House I had the strange impression that I was entering some sort of prison. The tall, spiked metal gates at the end of the long drive, the large wooden shutters on the windows, and the forbidding sturdiness of the house itself all combined to make me feel somewhat uneasy. The morning was, I must admit, dank and dismal with a heavy fog, and the tall bushes in the grounds dripped and drooped miserably with moisture; so I suppose my impression had its roots in some emotional well-spring rather than in any objective assimilation of what I saw.

Lord Brandon himself greeted me cheerfully enough, and once inside the warmth of his fire-lit drawing-room I began to feel comfortable again. My employer was a chubby man with kindly eyes and a jovial manner, not at all the kind of person one would expect to have fathered so strange and unusual a brood of children as he had (though perhaps I am gun-jumping a bit here: it wasn't until much later that I began to think of them as at all strange or unusual), and he welcomed me more as a visiting relative than a tutor lately arrived at his place of employment.

My job was to teach the children the rudiments of English, mathematics and science, and when I asked about their coaching in other subjects, Lord Brandon looked at me in surprise.

'Oh, didn't I tell you?' he asked cheerfully, leaning forward in his chair. 'You have a colleague, a second tutor whom I have hired to teach my children the subjects you do not yourself specialize in. He arrived late last night and began his duties this morning.' Lord Brandon looked at his watch. 'He is with the children now, but he should be finishing soon. I will introduce you and afterwards you can meet your pupils.'

I nodded and smiled, and I sat back to enjoy the drink my employer insisted I should have to warm me on this cold and miserable day. Presently my new colleague entered the room.

John Graydon was a pleasant young man, tall and dark with a huge drooping moustache which seemed to belie the cheerfulness that constantly shone in his eyes. His handshake was firm and dry.

'Glad to know you, Mr Ryan,' he said.

'Please,' I protested. 'If we are going to be colleagues, then we must know each other by our Christian names. Mine is David.'

He smiled and nodded, and then looked at Lord Brandon who had been watching us with what could almost be described as detached amusement. Our employer came forward and placed a hand on my shoulder.

'Come, David,' he said. 'Now that you have been introduced to your colleague, it's time for you to meet the children and begin your duties.'

I followed him out into the hall and up the wide staircase.

When I entered the nursery I was more than a little shocked. The room, although quite large, was a dark, cheerless place. Instead of bright wallpaper depicting various fairy-tale scenes, which was the usual decoration for the nurseries of children of the wealthy, I was greeted by dull brown walls, black paintwork, and small windows with dark and heavy curtains. The children, a quartet of cherubic, fair-haired innocents, were seated in a semi-circle in the centre of the room.

One by one, my employer introduced me to his offspring. Michael, the eldest, was a courteous young man of ten years. His smile was wide and completely disarming, as was Sandra's, his taciturn nine-year-old sister, who wore long blonde pigtails and had beautifully dimpled cheeks. Equally shy was seven-year-old Philip, while Jane, a little girl of six, seemed to be the most talkative and most tireless of all four. Every one of them was given to easy laughter, and every one of them possessed eyes of the brightest blue I had seen in a long while. I instantly fell in love with them all.

Lord Brandon watched with pleasure as they greeted me with enthusiasm, and I completely forgot to question him about the profound cheerlessness of their room. When, a day, or so later, I tackled him about it, he waved me away, somewhat irritably, telling me that the room was exactly how the children wanted it. At first I thought he was being ridiculous and was trying to dominate the children in a stupid sort of way by forcing them to work and play in their dismal nursery, and it wasn't until later that I realized I was gazing at a somewhat inverted picture; in fact the children were the ones who did all the dominating. Lord Brandon loved his offspring deeply and their wishes, much to my surprise, invariably overruled his.

Throughout the following weeks, however, my work went well and the children were charming. The lessons were wonderful two-way affairs in which I learnt just as much as my pupils. They told me about their mother, who had died two years previously, and I discovered that, surprisingly, none of them had any yearning to see what lay beyond the grounds of Brandon House: they were perfectly happy here and, playing in their make-believe worlds, they were content with life as they found it. John would take them for lessons in the mornings, and in the afternoons they would greet me with excited accounts of all they had learnt on that day. Little chubby-faced Jane would sit on my lap and chatter away into my amused ears, while the others sat cross-legged on the floor and laughed happily. Often during those weeks I would talk with John about it.

'They *are* a charming foursome,' he agreed on one dark evening when we were able to relax in our shared room. 'And they tell me all that you teach them as well as telling you all that goes on in my lessons. It's all very natural and they are happy and they play contentedly. And yet . . .' He shook his head and gazed at the floor, his drooping moustache like a bushy awning over his lower lip.

I frowned. 'Something's troubling you?'

'It's probably nothing,' he replied, smiling. 'It's just that I have this strange uneasiness inside of me, all the time.'

'Uneasiness? What about?'

He shrugged. 'The children. There's something not quite *right*, somewhere, don't you think?'

Sipping my sherry, I looked sideways at him. 'Oh, come on, John,' I scolded. 'Don't let the atmosphere of that nursery get you down so much . . .'

He shook his head again. 'It's not that.' He looked up at me. 'It's something to do with the children themselves, I *know* it is.'

I leaned forward and patted his shoulder. 'It's being confined in this house; that's what's wrong. Have another drink and forget all about it.' I lifted the bottle and waited for him to hold out his glass.

'I suppose you're right,' he said. But he was silent for the rest of the evening.

On the following afternoon the children were bouncing with excitement. The boys were wrestling good-naturedly on the floor when I walked into the room, and as I lifted little Jane in my arms, Sandra jumped up and down in front of me.

'Mr Graydon's been teaching us about "clubs",' she confided.

'Clubs?' I repeated, laughing. 'The kind you hit people with?'

'No, no! The kind that people join, of course!'

'That interesting,' I said, as Jane began to play with my ears.

Sandra clapped her hands. 'So now we've formed our own club. It's very secret. The four of us children are members and so is Mr Graydon and so is you.'

'"And so *are* you",' I corrected, but she went on as if she hadn't heard.

'We've called it the Nursery Club, and no one is to know about it. Not even Father. It's very, very secret.'

I smiled. Good for John. At least he was doing something to raise himself out of his depression. This club thing of his was a good idea; the children were bubbling over with enthusiasm. When next I spoke to him I told John how much I agreed with it.

'I was teaching them something about history,' he told me

'when somehow I got on to the subject of clubs, and it came naturally from there.' He smiled, his eyes shining again.

'How on earth did you get on to the subject of clubs when you were talking about history?' I asked. 'Surely you weren't teaching children of that age about the Hell-Fire Club.'

He laughed. 'My dear fellow, of course I wasn't!' He shook his head. 'I can't remember exactly how I *did* become side-tracked, but I shall be resuming the history part tomorrow.'

And so he did. But somehow, it seemed to me, he had been side-tracked again.

'We've been learning all about traitors,' Philip told me with seven-year-old eagerness on the next afternoon. 'Do you know what they did to traitors in the old days?'

Inwardly I was frowning, but I tried not to show it as I smiled down at him. After all, every little boy goes through a stage of fascination with morbid subjects. 'They executed them, didn't they?' I answered.

'Yes,' he said, smiling. 'They cut off their heads. But do you know what they did afterwards?'

This time I shuddered. 'Please be quiet, Philip. And let's get on with our arithmetic lesson, shall we?'

For the next two hours the children followed their studies in a somewhat uneasy silence. Young Philip was positively sullen. For the first time I became aware of something unnatural about them, a feeling of not-quite-rightness; the same thing, I suppose, that John had felt.

Afterwards I told him about it.

'Oh, forget it,' he told me. 'I got over it and there's no doubt that you will.' He laughed and ran his tongue along the bottom of his moustache. 'Come on, let's go down to the village and get merry; it'll be Christmas in a couple of weeks and everybody'll be in the mood.'

I picked up the bottle that was on the table and held it up to the light.

'I don't think we should,' I told him. 'You've drunk almost two-thirds of this as it is.'

He grinned. 'That's all right. Lord Brandon doesn't mind.'

'That's not the point.' I gave him a straight look.

He laughed and leaned back on his bed. 'I told him about the children's club today. He thought it was a good idea too.'

I pursed my lips. 'You shouldn't have done that. The children wanted their club to be a closely guarded secret; they'll be very disappointed.'

John waved me to silence. 'That's all right. After all, it's only a make-believe thing; it serves no real purpose.'

'It serves a *very* good purpose,' I assured him. 'If it holds the children's interest and imagination, then that's more than enough.'

'Oh, you worry too much,' he replied, laughing.

I shrugged. 'I hope you're right. It'd be a very great shame to waste such a good idea.'

The following morning was dark and dismal. A heavy fog had settled over the grounds; a fog which seemed thicker than any I had known before. Moisture dripped from everywhere, just as it had done on the day of my arrival, and every corner of the house seemed dark and cold despite the roaring fires that crackled with devilish fury in almost every room. I had slept uneasily during the night, and when I went to begin the afternoon's lesson I was feeling more than a little depressed.

The children were quiet and sullen.

'Why, whatever's the matter?' I forced myself to be cheerful. 'You all look very morose.'

Sandra looked up at me, sadly. 'It's Mr Graydon. He told Father about our club.'

So that was it! I cursed inwardly. John had to go and open his mouth. I would have the devil of a job keeping them happy this afternoon.

'Never mind,' I said, smiling. 'I've got some nice things for us to do today.'

Suddenly I stopped as I noticed the spot of blood on the floor.

I whirled round, angrily. 'All right!' I demanded. 'Which one of you has been playing with a knife?'

They shook their heads in silent unison. Their eyes seemed to shine like blue flames in their porcelain-white faces. My skull seemed to suddenly shrink and a shiver of horror ran like a spider up my back. All across the far wall of the room was a dark smear of blood.

'Mr Graydon betrayed our club,' Sandra explained with quiet patience. 'He was a traitor.'

Was? Did she say *was*? I backed away instinctively. My mouth hung open and my eyes were wide. I lifted a trembling hand.

'What have you done?' I managed at last to whisper. 'Oh, my loving God, what *have* you done?'

They were all smiling now. 'You know what they did to traitors in the old days, don't you?' Philip said.

I gaped at them, silently; and then, for the first time, I noticed the large knife in Michael's hand.

'Oh, my God!' I muttered to myself. No longer were they four innocents: now I could *see* the unnaturalness in their faces; the devil's light burning in their insane eyes. I turned, scrabbling for the door handle.

Behind me they were yelling: 'He was a traitor! He was a traitor!'

I flew down the dark staircase, stumbling and falling. Oh my God, oh my God, oh my God. 'Lord Brandon!' I yelled hoarsely into the dark empty rooms. 'Lord Brandon! Lord Brandon!' I leapt for the front door. It was stiff. I pulled and it came open. I stumbled out into the cold wet fog. The afternoon was incredibly dark, like a winter's evening. I leaned against the doorpost, panting heavily. Behind me I could hear four pairs of tiny feet thudding down the staircase. Closing my eyes, I wanted to say: 'I'm not a traitor, I'm not a traitor,' but I was dizzy with panic and I stumbled forward, falling on to the gravel of the forecourt. In my mind I could see Philip's laughing face saying: 'Yes, they cut off their heads. But do you know what they did afterwards?'

I scrambled to my feet and ran into the fog. But do you know what they did afterwards? But do you know what they did afterwards? The phrase kept pounding through my head as I ran. The dark fog was all around me, clinging against my skin like clammy fingers and pushing itself up into my nostrils. My feet crunched on the gravel of the drive.

Yes, I knew what they did afterwards. They took the traitor's head and impaled it on one of the spikes of Traitor's Gate.

And there was a spiked gate here, too!

I ran through the damp darkness. Oh, please God, no! Don't let it be what I'm thinking, please!

I ran on down the drive and suddenly the bars of the metal gate loomed ahead. I was afraid to look up. I collapsed against it, grasping the cold, sticky metal.

Sticky!

I felt the stickiness on my hands, a stickiness that could not have been caused by the fog alone. But it could have been caused by a combination of fog and . . .

I closed my eyes, too afraid to look at my hands and see the colour of the stickiness; too afraid to look up in case I saw the head of the traitor, the shining eyes for ever dulled, the drooping moustache . . .

Behind me, four pairs of tiny footsteps sounded on the gravel.

Laura

Barry Martin

I love Laura. I'll always love her.

She hasn't been at all well lately. Not since, the accident. I'm afraid that she thinks it was my fault, but she hasn't said anything. She wouldn't say anything that would hurt me. She loves me. Just as I love her.

Yes, I'll tell you about it, if you like. It was night when it happened. About three weeks ago – around 11.30. We were driving home from Bob's place. It was Joyce's birthday and they had asked us over for a drink.

Oh yes, I had been drinking. Not a lot. Not enough to make me lose control of the car. It was raining, I remember, and very cold out. We had the car heater on, and the radio. Laura was humming to the tune they were playing, tapping her foot to the rhythm, when suddenly she screamed, very loudly, 'Jack, for Christ's sake be careful!' And then it happened – the thud, the smashing of glass and Laura's screaming mingling into the blackness.

She hasn't spoken to me since. Oh no, we haven't had a row or anything. Please don't think that. We've never argued since we've been married – except for the time I dropped my cigarette and burnt a hole in the dining-room carpet – but we didn't argue for long. I told you – we love each other. She loves me and I love her. I'll always love her.

Why hasn't she spoken to me? It was the shock – of the accident. It took her speech away. It does that, you know, and then, without warning, it comes back – just like that. Very soon, when she has recovered, she'll speak to me again. She'll throw her arms around me and tell me just how much she loves me.

Laura was so lively before, that to see her now upsets me, very much. I lift her out of bed, dress her and sit her up in the chair by the window in the bedroom. I don't do this very often as I'm afraid she may catch cold. At night, as I climb into bed beside her, I kiss her gently on the cheek and tell her that she will soon be well again.

A doctor? No! I will call no doctors. They will try to take Laura away from me again. Like they did before – just after the accident. They said it would be better for both of us if they took her away. Stupid bastards! How can they say what's good for us and what isn't?

I got her back though. I found out where they had taken her and brought her home. I want her here with me. When you love someone as much as I love Laura, you'll realize how much it means to me to have her here, just sitting beside her and holding her hand.

Nobody comes to see her now. A few people come to see me, but they never mention Laura. They're afraid of upsetting me. I never bring her down when they're here. She doesn't need other people's company. She needs only me and my love and affection.

She will soon be well again. Then it will be just like old times – eating hot-snack suppers in front of the fire, going for walks in the park and making love in the darkness of the bedroom.

Laura is a wonderful lover. She has a warm, all-engrossing body that moves in a steady rhythm with mine. Smooth, milk-white breasts, her nipples erect, pressing into the palms of my hands like hard little buds. Her pretty red lips touching mine. Her tongue searching my mouth. Her fingernails scratching my back as we reach the climax of our love.

And then she would throw her arms around my neck. 'Darling, I love you so,' she would say. And I would look at her. Look into her Stygian-black eyes. Dark eyes. As dark as night.

As dark as it was on the night of the accident. As dark as it was on the night, a week later, when I dug Laura's body up from the graveyard and brought her home.

I love Laura. I'll always love her – always.

The Dancing Shoes

Rachel Kemper

They had always fascinated her, those white ballet shoes lying on black velvet in the window of the little shop in the narrow, crooked street. They seemed to be made, not of satin and steel and stitched, heavy lining, but of opalescent dreams, spun-sugar thoughts, and the essence of a Dégas painting. Every evening, returning home from the tall steel tower where she worked all day over a clattering typewriter, she would pass the shop, and always she would pause and look at the slippers.

The satin of them – how white it was! It seemed to half absorb, half reflect the tints of the other shoes that were neatly arranged in a circle about them. The brilliantly coloured shoes were like a varicoloured necklace, with the delicately lovely white slippers placed carefully, even reverently, in the centre. Resting so lightly on the black velvet, the shoes seemed scarcely to touch it; indeed, the shimmer of the satin increased this illusion so that the shoes seemed to hover over the velvet like restless butter-flies. Visible colour rays seemed to flash from the narrow ribbons, themselves devoid of colour, as they curled indolently over the soft black cloth. Even as they lay there, the shoes seemed to cry out for dancing feet, strong muscular feet, feet that would whirl to mad, wild music, or glide to a sweet melody while the gentle notes fell about them like pale pink flowers as the feet would dance on . . . and on.

Alive! That was the word for them – those shoes that be-witched the eye and enslaved the heart. Who that had seen them could keep from wanting them? There was almost an actual magnetic pull from them, and as she continued to stare at them, she could see herself in a fluffy white dress, following with graceful arms and pliant body the lilt and fall of a Tchaikovsky waltz or the subtle rhythms of a Chopin nocturne. And always, when she saw her image in the clear plateglass, the wonderful dream dissolved, the music faded, and only the shoes remained, magical and terrible on the black velvet.

She would sigh then, and pass on, for slippers and dancing were not for her. And even as she finally felt the chill and slush of the winter day, she would curse herself for her foolishness – gawking over a pair of ballet shoes, merely because as a child she had wanted to dance.

The sunset-haired girl across the street had gone to dancing school, and so had the blue-eyed girl whose parents were dreadfully rich, but she hadn't been able to go. Tears and pleas were no use. 'We haven't the money,' her father would say, 'and even if we had – I'm not sure I'd approve.' And that was that.

So now she mooned over a pair of common, ordinary ballet slippers in the window of an obscure little shop. Idiot! Idiot! Idiot! Her heels drummed the refrain as she ran up the stairs to her modest apartment.

But they weren't common – nor ordinary. They were everything she had ever hoped for, all she had ever wanted. They were both a symbol and a promise; a sacrificial altar to an old desire, and the doorway to a new one. She even went so far as to pretend that they were enchanted; that whoever wore them could dance, that the shoes would teach them. No matter how plain and awkward and drab she really was, she had only to think of the shoes to become another person, the one she had always wanted to be.

Of course, when she had come to the city, and at last held the necessary money, she had asked concerning this old dream. One day she had gone to the tall tower, and going from one vast mirror-lined room to another, she had talked to the understanding men and women and, knowing what to expect, she had not been hurt by their smiles. One did not begin to dance at her age, and there was the end of it. Yet, they had said, there are other jobs, our office, perhaps. So now there was the typewriter, a dull task really, but through her opened door she could hear the shouts of the ballet masters raised in various stages of infuriation at their pupils.

And then too, every evening when her work was done, she would go through the many rooms of the building and watch the dancers, sometimes on the great stage before an acre of empty seats, sometimes in small practice rooms, taking into herself the passion, fire and beauty of the dance, the crystalline purity and precision of it.

It was in a large, bare practice room on the top floor that she came upon the dark-haired man dancing alone to the music of a gramophone. Fascinated, she watched as he leaped and twisted to the pulsing dances from *Prince Igor* – violent pagan music that crashed about the room, hammered at the walls, and poured out through the large open windows.

Never had she seen dancing like this! There was a quality to it that she could not explain. Fierce, almost frantic emotion crept over her as she watched, half frightened, half bewitched. A queer aura of mystery seemed to hang over the whole room; native to the dancer, the music, and the dance itself, but quite foreign to the ballet school. Only when the music stopped and he turned to smile at her could she find enough will to slip out in sudden confusion and fright.

She came back the next evening to find him there again; and since he smiled so kindly, she came back many times to watch him, for who else in the great city ever found time to smile at an inconspicuous typist? The people of the city have no time for casual kindnesses.

At first, it was like rubbing salt in old wounds, for as his lithe, strong body flashed about the room, she twisted inwardly while she painfully felt her own inadequacy. Eventually, she stayed to talk with him – and found that he was as starved for friendship as she herself was.

His eyes were incredibly kind and sympathetic. They never mocked her, not even when she told him of the enchanted ballet shoes, and of her unrealized ambition to dance. His eyes were queer, too. Sometimes they seemed to be dark blue; sometimes they seemed to be black – compromising with herself, she finally called them violet. Before long, she thought of him only as the violet-eyed dancer. Once he had told her his name, but she had forgotten it, and was ashamed to ask again.

The weeks slid by like a harp *glissando*, and every evening she would watch him dance, and every evening she would pause a few moments to dream over the wonderful white ballet shoes. Sometimes the shopkeeper, a bent, gnarled old man, would wave to her, and she would absently wave back before returning to her apartment and a cup of hot tea.

And then, one evening in early spring when the last snow was still a soft slush on the sidewalks, she felt a warm hand on her shoulder, as she stood with her nose pressed against the glass that separated her from the shoes. Looking up in surprise, she met the violet eyes of her friend. He was smiling.

'Why don't you buy them?' he asked.

Buy them! She had never considered that. Buy them? Could such creations be had for money? The idea was unthinkable! But even as she stood there, half shocked, he had gone into the shop and the shoes were taken from the window. He was still smiling when he handed them to her, and she stammered confused thanks.

'They are yours, but I warn you, they're bewitched. You'll dance in them as no one has ever danced before, but you'll never walk again. Once on, they can never be removed, and the shoes will take you away with them.'

She laughed, and so did he. He was joking, of course, teasing her because of her wild fancy about the shoes. A sudden clear view of the facts made her mania seem ridiculous. She had merely wanted a pair of white ballet slippers for which she had no earthly use; and now that she had them, she didn't know what to do with them. So, laughing, hand in hand, she and the dark-eyed dancer walked down the street together; and, still laughing, she turned off into her apartment house, waving at him as she sped up the stairs.

After reaching her room, she unwrapped the shoes and examined them. The satin felt cool and slick to her nervous hands, and the ribbons twined about her wrists. Ordinary ballet slippers – again and again she tried to convince herself of their normality, but each time she failed miserably.

In sudden eagerness to try them on, she kicked her highly serviceable walking shoes across the room, and was ready to thrust her foot into one of the satin slippers when the telephone jangled loudly. Wrong number! Impatiently she clattered the phone back into the cradle, becoming unreasonably angry with herself as she realized her agitation.

Reluctantly, she packed the shoes away in her wardrobe. It would never do to dance while she was upset. Enchanted or not, the shoes would give but poor results if she was as jumpy as a cat.

In the days that followed, she found no chance even to look at the shoes. Her typewriter rattled incessantly as the new production, *Ballet of the Four Freedoms*, swung into full tilt. Letter after letter poured over her carriage roll: letters to shoe manufacturers, stage designers, orchestra conductors, letters to anyone and everyone whose services were needed to help make up one of the super-spectacles for which the Ballet Municiple was famous. There was so much to do, so much work; she came home tired every evening, and the shoes lay untouched in the wardrobe.

Also, during this time, she saw but little of her strange friend; yet, if she found a spare moment to run up to the practice room, he would be there, dancing alone to the little gramophone.

The night of the world première of the ballet was too much for her. To escape the vicarious tension, nervousness, and stage fright, she sought the practice room where she had so often watched her quiet friend as he danced. The precious ballet shoes were in a box under her arm, together with a dainty formal dress filched from the *Swan Lake* costumes. Half frantic with a desire at last to try her shoes, she cursed the slowness of the elevator as it hummed smoothly past wardrobe rooms, practice rooms, the tiny cubicles where the *costumiers* sat over yards of satin and tulle, up to the barn-like top of the great steel tower.

The top floor was quiet and deserted at this hour as she made her way to the practice room. Hesitating a moment before the door, she suddenly wanted to turn and run back down the hall, into the elevator, and back to the gay, warm backstage world where the little ballerinas awaited their grand entrances.

Gripping the doorknob as her panic subsided, she became

coldly furious with herself; she had come this far, and there was no use stopping now. She owed it to herself to overcome her crazy passion once and for all. Once she realized that she could not dance, with or without the shoes, then this nonsense would be over for ever. Far better to destroy your life's dream than to have it destroy you!

The door opened easily, and as easily closed behind her. Almost automatically she locked it, and hung the key over the doorknob by the long chain fastened to it. Quickly in that bare, cold room she plunged into the purloined dancing costume, while the mirrored walls mocked her stiff movements. And, at last, the moment she had lived for through these past months, she put on the shoes.

They fitted perfectly. It didn't surprise her; somehow she had expected them to fit. Lacing them tightly around her ankles, she waited for something to happen; but although she waited patiently, hopefully, the shoes gave no sign of life. Something seemed to die within her, although she desperately told herself that this was right, this was as it should be, that shoes were shoes, and nothing more. No shoes, however pretty and captivating they seemed in a shop window, could teach untaught feet to dance; they could not make her stiff body bend gracefully, or her awkward legs execute steps of which she knew nothing.

Still, to seal away for ever any belief in charmed shoes, she rose unsteadily to her feet, and tried to remember as much as she could of the various positions and steps.

It was no use. Simply no use. She had better tear off the dress and the shoes and run back to the typewriter. That at least she could manage. As she struggled with the knots in the ribbons, she heard a familiar voice, his voice.

'They don't work?' he asked.

'They don't work,' and she managed to laugh.

'Perhaps you went at it wrong.' He smiled in his queer way. 'For one thing, you have no music. And standing posturing before a mirror is no good either.'

'That's how everyone else learns.'

'But they do not have magic shoes.'

'Oh,' and, defensively, she put on a bantering tone of voice,

'It's not that I don't believe you, only that it has been a long time since the days of magic. I haven't heard of a case of good old-fashioned sorcery for quite a while.'

'Nor I; but you are lonely, and I am lonely, and the world has forgotten both of us.' He hunted among a stack of records, selected one, and put it on the gramophone.

'Come, dance with me; see, I'll show you!'

Her answering laugh was bitter, but she rose and took his hand and let him guide her around the floor. At first slowly, then faster and faster, the shoes pulled her feet in a strange pattern, around, around again. Over the music she heard him shout, 'You see, they are magic!'

They were! Her arms and body fell easily, effortlessly into the poised attitudes she had so often watched. The walls and floor fell away, and the only things remaining were the shoes and the violet eyes of the young man who held or released her while the music spun around them.

As they leaped together along the night wind, the light waltz became the harsh clangour of the stars in their circuits, while a thousand laughing demons shrieked at them from scarlet clouds. Waves of purple and gold swelled about them as the music became crystallized colour.

On and on she whirled, knowing the great, unholy joy of being that comes once to but few, and to no one twice. The one great dream of her life had become real, and she danced. All awkwardness and stiffness went from her, and her body became fluid, leaping with tireless legs, and bending and swaying in measured grace.

Wild and passionate, the barbaric music climbed to a climax; as the dark-eyed dancer grasped her for a great leap, they fell; her mouth opened to scream, but she could make no sound. The sky and space about her melted into a great sea of violet, and she clung blindly to his hands as the screaming stars clattered and crashed around them . . .

The policeman who found her the next morning grew poetically voluble over a drink in a nearby bar. 'Her face, good God, her face! Radiant it was, like the dawn on a clear morning, and her poor feet, so bare and bruised . . . Not another mark was there on her whole body . . . not a broken bone . . . yet falling all that distance! And falling on the exact spot where I found that other suicide just five years ago.

'Christ, I can see him yet; all twisted and broken, glaring at the heavens with those terrible, sightless violet eyes.'

The Peg-Doll

Rosemary Timperley

It all started in such a commonplace way. Alan came home from work as usual. He'd just completed a job for the demolition contractors who employed him.

'Look what I found on the site today,' he said to his wife.

She looked at the object in his hand. 'What is it?'

'A very old doll.'

The thing was hardly recognizable as a doll. There was a rough head and shoulders, the body tapering away to nothing, and no paintwork or features left.

'It must be at least a hundred years old,' he said. 'Claver Hall – that's the building we've just knocked down – used to be an orphanage in the nineteenth century. Maybe this belonged to one of the kids.'

'How fascinating.' Joan took the crude little doll into her hands and studied it. 'Is it worth anything?'

'I doubt it. I just thought Alma might like it.'

Joan laughed, for Alma, their seven-year-old daughter, was a most un-doll-loving child. Well-meaning friends and relations had given her pretty dolls at various times and she had treated them with disdain. They sat neglected in her toy cupboard.

Now the little girl came into the room. She was small, pale, black-haired and with beautiful brown eyes.

'What's that?' she asked immediately, looking at the object in her mother's hands.

'It's a very old doll, darling. Daddy found it at work. Would you like it?'

Alma stood looking cautiously at the doll, as if it were some strange animal. Then she put out her hand and touched it. She passed her fingers over the rough head and shoulders.

'I like her,' she said. 'Can I take her to bed with me?'

'Of course, darling.' Joan was pleased. Sometimes her daughter's unlovingness towards dolls had worried her. As a child herself, her dolls had been her beloved family.

So Alma took the doll to bed with her that night, and Alan and Joan laughed a little afterwards at the way their child despised her pretty fashionable, painted dolls, yet took this funny little peg-thing straight to her heart. She named it Rosalind.

The parents were less amused as the weeks passed and Alma, who took Rosalind with her wherever she went, became quiet and nervous during the day, and sometimes had bad dreams at night. It was Joan who first connected the change in Alma with the doll. 'It's uncanny the way she won't be without it,' she said to Alan. 'And I don't like the way she insists on taking it to bed with her.'

Alan said: 'Nonsense. What child hasn't taken a toy to bed at some time?'

'A teddy-bear, or a pretty doll, maybe,' said Joan, 'but that thing – it's beginning to give me the creeps.'

And it was during this conversation that Alma screamed out in the night. Joan dashed up to the bedroom. Alma was saying, sobbingly:

'I didn't mean to be naughty. Don't hurt me any more. Stop!'

And she was talking in her sleep.

Joan didn't wake her. She put her hand on the child's hair and said: 'It's all right, darling.' Alma quietened but did not wake.

Alan was in the bedroom now, standing just behind Joan, who whispered: 'I'm going to take that doll away from her.'

Gently, cautiously, she drew back the bedclothes, saw the doll enclosed in Alma's hands, and tried to take it.

Alma screamed, then said: 'No – no – I'll do anything if you let me keep her – I won't eat for a week – I promise —'

'For God's sake give it back to her,' said Alan.

So Joan stopped trying to take the doll, covered her daughter up again, watched her relax into quiet sleep, then the parents crept out of the room.

'What are we going to do?' Joan asked her husband.

'A child's nightmare —'

'It has something to do with that damned doll. We must find out more about it – where it came from —'

'You know where it came from.'

'We must find someone who knows about old dolls.'

This was more easily said than done, but they read an article in a magazine by a certain Miss Letherington, who called herself a 'plangonologist', collected dolls as a hobby, and knew a lot about them.

So Alan wrote to Miss Letherington, care of the magazine, and asked if he might have her address and come and see her. Her reply was an almost illegible scrawl, but he did get the address and went round there, taking the doll with him. This had not been easy, and he had felt guilty doing it – waiting for a moment when Alma left Rosalind for a second on a chair, turned her back – and then he had grabbed the doll and set out, leaving Joan to comfort the child.

Miss Letherington lived in a bedsitting-room full of dolls. They were of all nationalities, costumes and ages. They crowded together on her bed, her bookshelves, her chairs and on the floor. Miss Letherington was rather like a doll herself. She was neatly made and blank of face.

'Do come in,' she said to Alan. 'But don't disturb my darlings.'

Her 'darlings' gazed at him imperviously with glass eyes or empty sockets.

'Thank you for your letter,' she said. 'Have you brought me another darling for my collection?'

'I'm afraid not,' said Alan. 'It's your advice I want. Would you look at this doll and tell me what you can about it?' He held out Rosalind. The woman took it into her hands as if it were a living child, so gentle she was.

'Old,' she murmured. 'Full of pain. Much suffering.' Then she added in a more practical voice: 'These wooden peg-dolls were very popular in the nineteenth century. I have a similar one and it's 1850. It's rare to have one today, but they were cheap little toys at the time.'

'You don't find it sinister?' said Alan.

'No. Only sad. It's not a witchcraft doll. Not many of them

survive because they were made of wax – right for sticking pins into.'

'So it's just an ordinary old peg-doll,' said Alan.

'No doll is ordinary,' she reproved him. 'All are exciting and individual. I am never sure whether they have characters of their own, or whether they have absorbed the character of some-one who has loved them. Where did you find this child?'

'In the ruins of Claver Hall. It used to be an orphanage.'

'And once it was a pretty, gay, painted little doll, and someone loved it.'

'My daughter loves it. That's the trouble.'

'Nonsense,' said Miss Letherington. 'If your daughter loves this doll, it shows what a sensible girl she is. So many children nowadays fancy dolls in blonde wigs and bikinis with coy expressions.'

'Alma, my daughter, has been behaving strangely ever since she had this doll.'

'Perhaps she senses its suffering – or the suffering of someone who once owned it.'

'But what suffering? Can't you help me?'

Miss Letherington shook her head. 'When there is pain in a doll, I feel it,' she said. 'But the cause of the pain eludes me. Dolls are my children, and no parent ever really knows what is going on in the children's minds. The mind is a secret place.' Her voice drifted off. She looked round at her 'darlings'. 'I know which is happy and which is sad and which is unfeeling, but I never know why,' she added. 'Like any parent.'

Alan was shivering. With the cool, businesslike part of his mind he thought all this was a load of nonsense – and yet —

'What shall I do?' he said.

'Try to find out *why* the poor little thing was so unhappy,' said Miss Letherington, quite brusquely. 'Learn more about that orphanage, Claver Hall. And if your daughter could be persuaded to part with this dear little child, who has suffered so much, then I'd be delighted to have her in my collection.'

Alan stuffed Rosalind back into his pocket and left. He went to the public library, which seemed beautifully sane and down-to-earth contrasted against the doll-infested claustrophobia of

Miss Letherington's bedsitter. He found a book on nineteenth-century orphanages. 'Claver Hall' was in the index. And as he read the relevant pages, he wondered why he hadn't had the sense to do it before – even before that demolition job in which he had organized the building's destruction.

He read: 'Claver Hall was like other orphanages of the period – cold, uncomfortable, short of funds. The children's welfare depended on the personal qualities of those in charge. Often these were not suitable people – as Charles Dickens has shown us. However, Claver Hall ran smoothly enough, except for an unpleasant episode between 1857 and 1860. During this time, a widow called Grace Webb was in charge. She starved the children to line her own pockets. She terrorized them, punished them for "eating too much", and one of her punishments is said to be that she would take away the children's dolls if they were "naughty" or "ate too much". During those three years of Mrs Webb's rule, so many children escaped by either running away or dying, that even the negligent local authorities became suspicious, and Claver Hall was investigated. As a result, Mrs Webb was put in jail, where she died five years later. According to the records, she went mad before she died, believing herself to be haunted by dead children.'

Alan went home, the doll heavy in his pocket.

'Have you got Rosalind?' was the first thing Joan asked him. 'Alma's been wandering about all day looking for her, like a little ghost.'

And Alma came in. 'Daddy, did you take her?'

'Take whom?' he said.

'Rosalind, of course.'

'Why should I?'

'She's gone. I can't find her.'

'Perhaps she wanted to go away.' And he felt the doll hard against him in his pocket.

'I wouldn't mind not eating anything ever again if she came back,' said Alma, and wandered out again, to continue her search.

Alan told Joan what Miss Letherington had said, and what he'd read at the library. And he drew the peg-doll out of his pocket.

'We must get rid of her,' said Joan. She took the doll out of Alan's hands. 'It's nothing,' she said. 'Only a bit of old wood. Nothing. When I first saw it, I didn't even recognize it as a doll. Remember?' She passed her fingers over the rough head and shoulders. Pain shot through her fingers. A bright fire was burning in the grate. To get rid of the pain in her hands as much as anything else, she flung the peg-doll into the fire.

An unearthly voice cried: 'You're cruel! I hate you! You're cruel! You're cruel!' And, somewhere, Alma screamed.

Alan and Joan were never to know whether Alma had spoken those words before she screamed, or whether it was some other child's voice entirely.

Alma, still screaming, ran into the room. She knelt down before the brightly blazing fire. She called: 'Rosalind!'

And although the fire was burning brightly, so very brightly, the room was cold as death.

Man With a Knife

T. H. McCormick

You never become used to it.

As soon as I entered, the pungent odour of anaesthetic and antiseptic got me by the throat.

The attendant was getting ready to take the lift upwards, and I caught it just in time.

'Mr Kershaw's unit?'

'Seventh floor.'

He watched me curiously as we went up, evidently wondering where I was going to fit into the hospital.

I walked along the corridor, passed a door marked 'Mr Reginald V. Kershaw, MS', and almost bumped into the ward sister as I rounded the corridor.

She was plump and neat, with a fringe of white hair.

'Yes?'

'Sorry,' I said. 'I'm Frank Jackson, and I . . .'

'So you're the new house surgeon. Good.' She shook hands. 'I'm Sister Mackenzie. Come along and I'll show you round.'

We stood at the door, and looked down the ward. It was bright and airy. Newspapers and magazines on the centre table, several vases of flowers.

'This is a general surgical ward,' she said. 'Piped oxygen. The drugs cupboard is over there. Admission day is every Wednesday; the Chief examines the patients, and decides what to do, on Thursday. Friday is operating day.'

'What about casualty reception?'

'Once every ten days.'

It sounded good.

'I ought to get a good deal of experience here.'

Sister Mackenzie nodded. 'Mr Kershaw's an excellent surgeon,' she said. 'Of course, he's never been the same after his son died.'

I looked at her curiously.

'Oh dear, I shouldn't have said that. I hate gossip.' She paused awkwardly for a moment. 'It was a terrible emotional shock but his work wasn't affected. He's still a brilliant surgeon.'

'He should be.' I said. 'You don't get your Master of Surgery for nothing.'

There were four or five nurses in the ward, and she introduced them to me.

Then another one came in, and I forgot them immediately.

Slim, fair-haired, about twenty-four. Good figure, even under a nurse's uniform. Neat legs.

'This is Nurse Hartford. Liz Hartford.'

We shook hands. 'I hope you like it here,' I heard myself saying fatuously.

'I wouldn't think of working in any other ward.' She sounded very intense about it. Then she nodded politely, and went over to join one of the others in bedmaking.

I turned to Sister Mackenzie. 'It's a pity she's married,' I said, half jokingly.

'She's a widow.'

I hesitated. 'When did her husband . . .'

'Two years ago.' She looked embarrassed, and hesitated as if she was going to say something else. Then she turned as footsteps sounded in the corridor behind her. 'Here's Mr Kershaw,' she said, with obvious relief.

He was a tall man, about fifty, strongly built. He gave an impression of power and confidence.

'So you're Jackson?' he said, holding out his hand. 'Glad to have you with us.'

His grip was powerful.

Then he left me, to discuss someone's treatment with Sister Mackenzie.

It should be good, working with him, I thought.

It was.

Plenty of experience. Burns, scalds, fractures, appendixes,

crush syndrome, coronaries. It may sound unpleasant, but in fact it was exciting, with something new every day.

And there was Liz.

I watched her moving quickly through the ward, or seated at night at the desk, the shaded light shining on her fair hair as she marked up a pile of charts.

She knew I was watching, but pretended not to notice. Perhaps she thought I was looking for a quick hospital flirtation.

Then she came into the ward kitchen one day, when I was leaning against the wall, finishing a cup of coffee. Now or never, I thought.

'There's a good Peter Sellers film on at the Odeon tonight. Would you like to come?'

She looked surprised.

'Yes,' she said hesitantly. Then she collected herself. 'Yes, I would,' she said, more resolutely. 'Thank you.'

We walked home together, and I didn't kiss her goodnight. I wanted to, but I guessed it wasn't wise.

She thanked me pleasantly, but was a little withdrawn, a little cool.

For so young a girl, there seemed a lot of sadness behind her eyes. Give me time, I thought, and I would dispel it.

But it's never long before hospital idylls are interrupted by something grim.

A couple of weeks later, I met one of the orderlies coming along the corridor. Under his arm he had something long and lean, which was wrapped in a piece of sacking.

'What's that you've got, Charlie?'

'An amputation.'

I grimaced.

'It's an arm.' He patted it proudly. 'They say it was a real treat, the way the Chief took it off.'

We exchanged a few more sentences, then I went into the ward office. It had been admission day, and I'd to get the medical records ready for Thursday's rounds.

One of the patients was to get his appendix out, and I'd noticed earlier that he was wearing a cleverly made artificial arm. Idly, I wondered if he'd had it removed here.

I searched among the brown, manila envelopes till I found his, then started to read.

Edward Grey, machinist. Age, thirty-seven. Single. Measles at three years of age, mumps at eleven. Nothing else until six years ago, when his arm had been trapped in a piece of machinery. Severe laceration of left arm, comminuted fracture of left humerus. Arm amputated. Operation performed by R. V. Kershaw, MS.

So he *had* been one of our patients.

It seemed a pretty radical operation, even allowing for the fact that his arm had been broken in several places.

I looked for his X-ray plates. There were eight of them. I snapped them under the clips of the viewer, and switched on.

The white bone showed up immediately against the darker mass of the muscles. The break in the upper arm was clearly visible. A nasty fracture, but an operation, followed by putting it in plaster, should have been enough.

A senior houseman came in.

'What are you looking at, Frank?'

I told him, and he examined the plates. 'Hmm ... yes ... probably some complication set in. You'll find it in the case notes.'

'I didn't.'

'Then it must be somewhere else.' He looked at the plates again, then shrugged his shoulders. 'You won't forget, will you,' he said pointedly, 'that you'll have to have sixteen case histories ready for the Chief tomorrow?'

'I won't.'

I let it slip to the back of my mind.

Hardly surprising. The sheer day-to-day routine filled most of my time.

Going round the ward every morning. Taking notes. Writing up histories. Arranging for blood counts, X-rays, cardiograms, treatments.

Half the time I seemed to be hurrying somewhere, the other half I was on the telephone.

Sister Mackenzie and I hardly had time to do more than exchange rueful smiles, over the crowds who seemed to pour in and out of the place – patients, visitors, nurses, specialists, physiotherapists, dietitians, social workers of every kind.

Then a patient was transferred to us from another ward.

Charlie brought him in, and we stood chatting by the window, enjoying the sun on our backs.

'I hear your Chief was doing another amputation, this morning,' he said.

'An arm?' The word slipped out before I realized it.

He looked at me in surprise. 'How did you know?'

No time to check up on what I was thinking, because I was going out with Liz, but tomorrow night, I promised myself, I'd see . . .

It was ten o'clock when I came into the ward.

Sister Mackenzie looked up from the desk.

'I thought you'd finished for the day, Frank.'

'I've got a few cases to write up.'

She smiled. 'All right. There'll be a cup of coffee ready, when you've finished.'

'Thanks.'

I went into the office, and over to the records section marked 'Kershaw'. In one year, he must have done hundreds of operations. I was only looking for one particular kind, but it was going to be a long night.

Three hours later I put the last bundle of typewritten sheets down.

It was hardly believable . . . but true.

In more cases than could possibly be explained, he had removed an arm. Not in the very simple ones, certainly, but he'd done it again and again where nothing more than a straightforward operation was needed.

It seemed he had deliberately . . .

I tried to think if I'd heard any gossip or comment about it, but hadn't. You don't question a surgeon's decisions, any more than a private questions a general's.

There didn't seem to be any other explanations for the facts, and yet . . . Was I putting a lurid interpretation on something, for which there was a perfectly reasonable explanation? Had I missed something.

I pushed the papers aside, and went into the ward.

Sister Mackenzie was filling up the ward report. 'Goodness, you look tired. Let's go into the kitchen, and I'll make that coffee. Nurse Hartford can take over.'

Liz smiled as we passed, but I could hardly reply.

We sipped our coffee, and I steered the conversation round.

'Mr Kershaw? Oh yes, a fine man. Married, with two daughters. And then, of course, there was his son.' She stopped abruptly.

'Yes?' I said encouragingly.

She hesitated. 'You didn't hear anything about it?'

I shook my head.

'He was injured in a road accident near the hospital. They brought him in here. His arm was terribly damaged. It had to be removed, or he would have died. The Chief wanted to do it, and everyone tried to stop him.'

'Why?'

She looked surprised. 'Surgeons always send their own family to someone else. They're too emotionally involved.'

'And what happened?'

'He should never have done it,' she said vehemently. 'It was a mistake. It would have been all right, if it had been anyone else's son.' She shook her head. 'He took far too long. First a nerve was cut ... then an artery. There was ... blood everywhere. His son died on the table.'

And ever since he'd gone on repeating the operation.

'Poor devil,' I whispered.

Sister Mackenzie cleared her throat, reached across the table, then stopped.

'What on earth's the matter, Frank? You've spilled half your coffee.'

'It's all right,' I said, mopping it up. 'I've just remembered I'd got to see the Chief about something.'

'What's the hurry?' she asked. 'He'll be in shortly to see how that young child is doing.'

'Thanks, but it's ... rather urgent.'

I knew he would be taking the short cut through the spinney, and I didn't want what I had to say to develop into a shouting match.

It was quiet and dark as I began walking down the beaten earth path.

I was lucky. A couple of minutes later, I saw him striding towards me.

'Mr Kershaw.'

He peered at me.

'Yes?'

'There's something I must say to you.'

'What is it?' he asked sharply.

I started to tell him.

He lowered his head for a moment, then stepped forward, and drove his fist into my face. I was literally too surprised to move. Then he was at me like a tiger, smashing in more blows, grunting with the force behind them. I tried to call out. He doubled me up with a blow in the stomach. I sank to my knees, and he kicked me in the ribs. I brought my arm up to protect my face, and he kicked at it twice, savagely.

Something in it broke, and grated.

I screamed.

Darkness.

Darkness and light.

And whiteness.

Whiteness of walls, and ceiling.

And above all, warmth, and comfort, and drowsiness. Nothing worried me, nothing mattered. Somewhere at the back of my mind, there was a small, niggling remnant of fear, but it was overwhelmed by the pervading lethargy.

Through the long, woollen bedsocks I was wearing, I could feel two hot-water bottles. I rolled over, and felt the tapes on the gown press against my back.

I am in hospital, I thought calmly. I am going to have an operation.

A figure moved by the bedside, and I tried to speak. My mouth was parched.

'He's coming round, Sister,' the nurse called.

There was the rat-tat of sensible shoes down the ward, then Sister Mackenzie appeared.

'My, my,' she said. 'We *have* been having a time to ourselves, haven't we?'

Oh God, the awful jocularity of hospitals!

She lifted the case sheet from the end of the bed, studied it for a few moments, then laid it down.

'You'll be all right,' she said reassuringly. 'One of the nurses found you in the spinney. The police are searching the grounds now. They say you must have been attacked by some hooligans.' She shook her head. 'Anyway, try to get some rest now. You'll be going into the theatre soon; you've already had your pre-operative injection.'

I knew it. The morphine that was making me so drowsy, the atropine that had already dried my throat.

I tried to raise myself up in bed.

'Easy now,' she said, pressing me down gently. 'It's only a fractured humerus.'

'My . . . arm . . .'

'Yes. The left one.'

I tried desperately to speak, and only mumbled disjointed words from a slack mouth.

Sister Mackenzie listened, frowning, then shook her head.

'Oh dear,' she said, 'you've got a touch of concussion, too.'

I tried again.

'Liz . . . Liz . . .'

Her face cleared. 'You want Nurse Hartford? Oh, all right then, if you want to hold her hand.' She turned to go. 'But you'd better hurry up, if you've got anything to tell her.'

'Why?' I croaked.

'The Chief will have finished scrubbing up soon.'

The Chief!

Then Liz was hurrying down the ward, fair hair bobbing under her cap. 'Darling,' She bent down, and kissed me. There were tears in her eyes.

A few words at a time, I began to tell her what had happened.

The operating gown was damp with sweat when I'd finished.

She looked alarmed, and began to assemble a syringe hurriedly. 'Sister Mackenzie told me ... but I didn't realize you were so badly concussed. I've never heard anything so ridiculous.'

She dabbed my arm hurriedly with spirit, then inserted the syringe, and pressed the plunger home.

Wouldn't somebody listen to me?

Then there was a rumbling which became louder, and Charlie came in, wheeling a trolley.

'Frank Jackson, for surgery'. Then he looked at me. 'Blimey, it's you, Doctor,' he exclaimed. 'This is a real turn-up for the book.' He turned to Liz. 'Is he ready, Nurse?'

'Yes,' she said, in a muffled voice.

He brought the trolley up to the side of the bed, and together they rolled me on to it. He tucked the blankets round me, while Liz put the case notes and X-rays at the foot.

It must have been another injection of morphine she had given me. I was even more lethargic than before.

They began wheeling me towards the door.

Sister Mackenzie smiled encouragingly from her desk.

I wish she would help me, I thought calmly.

We were in the corridor.

How odd the lights seemed, when you were lying on your back. Why hadn't I noticed them before? I wanted to tell someone, but perhaps it didn't really matter.

They manoeuvred me out of the lift, along the corridor, and into the anaesthetic room.

Liz looked down at me, for a long moment. There were tears on her cheeks.

'I'll just see that everything is ready,' she said in a choked voice, and disappeared into the operating theatre.

Charlie cleared his throat embarrassedly.

'Nice girl,' he said. 'Tough time she's had, what with her husband dying a couple of years ago.' He looked down at me. ''Course you know who she is, don't you? Hartford's her maiden name. She's really Mrs Roger Kershaw. The Chief's her father-in-law.'

The doors of the operating theatre opened, and he stood there, in white cap, gown, gloves, mask, boots.

His eyes were glittering above the mask.

Help me, somebody!

GHOST AND HORROR IN PAN

A SELECTION OF POPULAR READING IN PAN